NOT

MY

PRESIDENT

Edited by Josh Gaines

FIRST PRINTING

Published by Thoughtcrime Press
thoughtcrimepress.com

Edited by Josh Gaines

Cover art by Molly Crabapple. Art originally appeared in Molly Crabapple's article on The Guardian, *'I am your horse!': 50 shades of Trump on the stump*. Her art can be found at mollycrabapple.com

Design and layout by Josh Gaines
Typeset in Bembo

ISBN-10: 0-9887167-3-9
ISBN-13: 978-0-9887167-3-5

Library of Congress Control Number: 2017914447

Printed on acid free paper in the United States of America

10 9 8 7 6 5 4 3 2 1

NOT MY PRESIDENT

THE ANTHOLOGY of DISSENT

For The Resistance

Contents

WHEN HATE WINS

Who Controls The Past Controls The Future

WHEN POLITICS ARE THICKER THAN BLOOD

No Vacancy

AMERICA.ru

Speak. Love. Fight.

MAKE THE NOISE YOU THOUGHT YOU COULD

NOT
MY
PRESIDENT

Jennifer Hudgens

Foul

 After Allen Ginsberg

America, why did Bob Dylan win the Nobel Prize for literature?
America, why are we rewinding to the 1940s?
America, will you collect enough corpses
to match Time Magazine's 1938 man of the year?

I would've smoked 1,149 cheap menthol cigarettes
in the last 76 days—I've saved two hundred and twenty-eight
dollars and eighteen cents.

America, when did I become middle-aged?
Get off my lawn you damned kids!

America, you piss me off with your lack of Jazz and Shakespeare in the
mall—I hate going to the mall unless it's for enchiladas on Wednesdays.
America, is Yellow Stone cannibalizing bodies—for beauty?

America, will my mother's dog stop licking his ass
long enough so I can eat my Greek yogurt in peace?
America, I'm tired of staring at assholes.
America, why is there a hipster nativity scene available only through Amazon?

Why do I only have one headlight and bald tires?
Thanks, America.

America, I'm watching you divide and devolve.
America, I thought we were better than this.
America, are we entering another holocaust?
America, I'm afraid.

America, can you turn our silhouettes into something
beautiful and reckless—fourth grade, gravel—skinned knees,
do you remember the time I caught a bee in my lunch box?
We were so innocent then, America.

America, when Gil Scott Heron said,
"The revolution will not be televised," was he right?
America, why are we unfolding?

America, I'm glad my father didn't live to see you like this.

America, Internet trolls think Cosby is innocent—Bukowski was a brilliant misogynist, and Neruda, a tyrant—admitted to raping a woman in his memoir—but America, he wrote the most beautiful poems.
America, why do some of the worst people make the best art?

America, how often do you wash your hands?
America, do you think brown girls are disposable?
America, we are grieving on the bones of slaves.
America, how do you sleep at night?
America, why is it so hard to get up in the morning?
America, why can't the natives have their lands back?

America, why do you treat your veterans like disabilities?
America, why are people with disabilities only good enough
for inspiration porn?
America, why do you love pornography so much?
America, why can't you stop uploading photos of your lunch to Instagram?
America, you are not a duck-billed platypus.
America, why are you Jenga and Tetris?

America, is the noise too loud?
America, is the music turned all the way up?
America, why can't you hear us trembling, our teeth chattering?

America, can I kiss girls and boys and swing high enough on the playground to break gravity—America, why is gravity so much like grieving?

America, are you listening?

Jennifer E. Hudgens was born & raised in Oklahoma. Jennifer uses poetry to navigate the weirdo/darkling/beautiful thing called life. Jennifer holds a Bachelors degree in English/Creative Writing from the University of Central Oklahoma & will be attending Oklahoma State University for her MFA beginning Aug. 2017. She is Editor in Chief at Wicked Banshee Press, Assistant Poetry Editor of Jazz Cigarette, and poetry reader at FIVE2ONE.

Jennifer has been published in several online and print journals. Jennifer has poems forthcoming in CrabFat Magazine, and FIVE2ONE in 2017. Jennifer's chapbook *Paloma*, will be released through Blood Pudding Press, and her 2016 full length collection *Girls Who Fell in Love With War* will be released as a second edition through Swimming With Elephants Publications later this year.

Jennifer is constantly striving to be a better human and poet.

WHEN HATE WINS

Election Eve

I.

Any longer I can only speak in prayer.
My mouth opens and my father the preacher finds fresh life.
Only I pray to everything—the cracked lamp,
the turned back clocks, the four stamps with Harvey Milk's grin
grinning like squares of witchcraft, the black globe on the bookshelf,
the fat pine cones, the still mute record player, the dew printed windows
who always answer my prayers with the same advice—
don't see, see-through.
I'm trying.
Most days it's like walking on the bottom of a swimming pool.
Like you're shouting from the surface and I hear you,
but it's like [underwater sounds].
I'm practicing with the deep. I've got to want it. I've got to push
down here, negotiating changes in gravity
to keep my instincts for the ground sharp.

II.

America, our chickens are coming home to roost,
but they're all fucked up.
They've been feeding on science fiction.
They've been eating zombies and robot rebellions
and the curdling screams of Sigourney Weaver
and now they are hungry for apocalypse.
They come up the driveway moblike,
like a sea of hairpieces out for blood.

III.

The Dalai Lama has weighed in from the land of forever mudras.
He's been eating the pink sugar skulls of lovingkindess.
He's replaced his asshole with warm light.
He speaks to the New York Times from beneath the giant ruby resting
on his chest and offers a simple transmission:
Behind the anxiety and uneasiness is a fear of being unneeded.
We hunger for our right place.
We hunger to be in service.
This is the most human hunger.
We want to light the fire for another's way, so that we might see our own.
The answer to all this pain and rage is not, finally, systemic.

It's personal—we must begin to appreciate the gifts of all others.
I picture myself trying to find the gift in Donald Trump,
but it keeps morphing into a vision where
I go to rip out his heart on national television
but find only a gold watch. The audience gasps.
Meanwhile drought.
Meanwhile despair gathers like dead needles on the forest floor.

IV.

Three days left and Nate Silver is crystal balling it.
The gods are lining up for our genuflecting:
Great Florida, wearing matching magenta capes with its wild haired children
Miami, Orlando, Pensacola, West Palm Beach, Jacksonville.
Holy Pennsylvania, munching mountain laurel on a pile of deer.
All powerful North Carolina, Michigan, Colorado, Virginia, Wisconsin.
Sublimest Iowa, Ohio, Minnesota, Nevada.
Please, be merciful.
May the lie detector tests of our collective guts
still know how to sound alarms in the time of free porn
and the time of reality TV and the time that trust left us.
Please. Please. Please. Please.
Please.

V.

Sister Hillary.
Grandmother with the good hair.
Grandmother who doesn't even know how to use a computer.
Grandmother Methodist.
Grandmother carved in the classrooms and courtrooms of petty men
drinking power in their dark blue suits.
Grandmother warrior pose.
Grandmother complexity.
I imagine your neural pathways, dense glittering city maps of knowledge
and lessons and experiences and all the hands you've shook and all the
bodies you've hugged and all the concern you've felt, pathways flooding
electric with relationship.
Grandmother come from the temples of bureaucracy with the wands of
policy and teamwork and repair and warm chiding.
Grandmother scaring the shit out of us.
Grandmother come to slay the myth of isolation.
I save my final morning prayers for you.
I try to sound perfect and righteous and start crying.
All the objects in the room lean in.

VI.

Sincerity is the only currency I bring.
On this eve of Eves, on this swell of tidings,
on this forking river of time, dice in the air, copper panic in the air,
all I have to do is stand here in my vulnerability and desire.
All I have to do is stand here with my whole heart.
I must not hold my breath, but rather, breathe.
Feet planted firmly on the ground.
Head gathering sun.
I am made of seeds.

Mindy Nettifee is an award-winning writer and performer. She is the author of two full-length poetry collections – *Sleepyhead Assassins* (Moon Tide Press) and *Rise of the Trust Fall* (Write Bloody Press), and a collection of essays on writing – *Glitter in the Blood* (Write Bloody Press), a Powell's Books Indie Press Best Seller. Her third collection *Open Your Mouth Like a Bell* is forthcoming on Write Bloody in the Spring 2018. She is currently a doctoral student in Depth Psychology and Somatic Studies, researching the impact of trauma on the voice and languaging. She also produces and hosts with the storytelling powers of The Moth and Back Fence PDX, and teaches classes at Literary Arts in Portland, OR. You can hear one of her stories on The Moth podcast, and visit her work online at thecultofmindy.com.

Pop Culture Politics

It was a long time coming/
a slow boil/ a witch hunt/
and then/ a certain kind
of electricity/

A girl balances, as if caught
in the middle of a dance, moves
her loose shoe back into place
under the dim streetlight, ignores
the catcalls and light applause,
slips her ring of keys
between her fingers
like a makeshift weapon.

It's just the way things are,
the way *all men talk/*
in/ locker rooms/ and to
each other. It's/ *boys*
being boys/ except,
of course,/ *not your husband*
or your son/

A girl gathers up her things,
exiled from her family's house
after a rape, spends years tied
to a table with thick shame-rope,
sees glass jars of her body
parts with labels that read
"wants attention," and "liked
it," and *"should have just kept*
her knees together."

You focus on the good/
stockpile Plan B/ get an IUD/
control your life/ make
Mike Pence cry/ after all/
men find young women
to be attractive sexually.
Put them together and/

A girl walking tugs the hem
of her dress over her knees
when cars go by, has 9-1
already dialed when she parks,
never looks away from her drink
at a party or on a date,
grows up to be called
a nasty woman, a devil
if she asks for a man's seat.

Eat it, Beyonce/ yes, do.
Sit mighty at your table
and know that a woman can
use her body to make more
bodies, to reshape the whole earth.

Anna Sandy is in the final year of her MFA in poetry at Georgia State University, where she also teaches English Composition. She is the current Editor in Chief of New South, and her work can be found in SFWP's The Quarterly, Santa Ana River Review, Muse/A, Nightjar Review, and others. She lives in Atlanta with her fiancé and three cats.

Global Gag Rule

A large man at a polished desk
flanked by a phalanx
who stand and watch
him ready his pen with swagger.

White skin, dark suits. No place
for our breasts, buttocks,
loins, legs, wombs, mouths, vulvas,
vaginas so dangerous

a wall of shoulders forms
behind the front, hands crossed
over crotches. No touching.
He signs the order, as if he could

silence the bodies bearing
riches of mischief and magic.

Grace Mattern has been published widely, including two books of poetry. She's received fellowships from the New Hampshire State Arts Council and Vermont Studio Center. For thirty five years she's been deeply involved in the movement to end violence against women. gracemattern.com

Too Much Screen Time - February 21
Geoffry Smalley

Five Days Before the Election

& I don't want to feel the earth today because a rich man is in it
who says he has the right to grab
the most *mine* thing I can think of but maybe wouldn't want to
because maybe I am almost thirty
& have grown stately in myself these last three years,
watched ass & breasts become
rounder worlds & said *okay, I can inhabit more*
cells, can be the earned size
of my grandmothers. & it is American to consider
that he has a right to lead
America, to gather the wrinkled hands of bankers
and show them all the nooks & crannies
cloaking hushed treasures, teach them how to strip
the quiet armor women don
when we are tired of eyes following our legs
up staircases. I want to lie
down in a river bed, to let the water rush over
until I am a cold nothing,
touched only in the urgent pity of rescue
divers dragging me
back to earth. I want to let a man, a stranger, worry
over my body, what makes it
tick & gasp. I want to name each thigh dimple
and raised vein, each flake
of dry skin & stubbled hair, lest someone think
they were ownerless,
run their hand up my skirt on a bus like it wasn't
a valued thing thieved. I want
to be precise about how rich I am, how bountiful
my folds of skin: this museum
of a pussy, this grand opera belly. Let the government
erect a fence around my yards
of legs, lush country of bush & blood. Let me be
a closed border, private country.

After the Election I Woke Up

covered in hives. Sometimes the body
refuses the day's story,
screams at the news in small places
that say *no, I will not*
consent to this invasion, I will fight
at my own risk, break
red, spill this little stream of blood
across clean sheets.
And this is what I have faith in:
the body's knowledge
of threats to its sovereignty. I can choose
dozens of products to lessen
my response to danger. I leave CVS
with bag full of gentle,
sensitive skin lotions and ointments.
It is good to be wrought tender
enough to feel the day's sting. Discomfort,
a warning: *stop this. Stop*
this before this whole body is a swollen open
sore, a wreckage of neglect.

Stevie Edwards is the founder and editor-in-chief of Muzzle Magazine and senior editor in book development at YesYes Books. Her first book, *Good Grief* (Write Bloody, 2012), received the Independent Publisher Book Awards Bronze in Poetry and the Devil's Kitchen Reading Award from Southern Illinois University, Carbondale. Her second book, *Humanly*, was released in 2015 by Small Doggies Press, and her chapbook, *Sadness Workshop*, is forthcoming from Button Poetry. She has an M.F.A. in poetry from Cornell University and is a Ph.D. candidate in creative writing at University of North Texas. Her writing is published and forthcoming in Crazyhorse, Indiana Review, TriQuarterly, Ploughshares Blog, Redivider, 32 Poems, Ninth Letter, The Journal, Rattle, Verse Daily, and elsewhere.

Lisa Markley

Pussy Hat

Pussy: (noun) a cat
as in *Pussycat, pussycat, where have you been?*

Women. You gotta treat 'em like shit.

Pick the most garish and girly shades of pink—
resist toughest tree-climbing, knee scraping,
tomboy rude-girl tendencies
when plundering your stash of stray yarns.
Choose the exotic, the sensuous,
the silks, the cashmeres, the baby alpacas.

*It must be a pretty picture
you dropping to your knees.*

Bind two contrasting pinks into single slipknot.

She got schlonged.

Efficacy: (noun) the power to produce the desired result.
See *gerrymander.*

*It doesn't matter what they write
as long as you've got a young
and beautiful piece of ass.*

Join the circle being careful not to twist the stitches.
Double-strand the knits and purls
in a two-by-two corrugated ribbing for 4 ¼ inches.

*You could see there was blood
coming out of her eyes,
coming out of her... wherever.*

Switch to stockinette stitch.
Alternate colors in horizontal stripes
until the piece reaches 9 inches from the cast-on edge.

How are her breasts?

Bind-off using Kitchener stitch.
Kitchener: (proper noun) a man who may
or may not have known how to knit.

*I have seen women manipulate men
with just a twitch of their eye
—or perhaps another body part.*

Weave in all loose tails.
Add a knit rose just below the ear
because *Hearts starve as well as bodies*

*The only thing she's got going
is the woman card.*

Your pussy hat is complete.
Freakin' Hello Kitty—take no shit.

Hope (noun) feeling of expectation
or desire for a certain thing to happen
as in *I hope these burglar bars hold
against the coming zombie apocalypse.*

Such a nasty woman.

*Women have one of the great
acts of all time;
the smart ones act
very feminine and needy,
but inside they are real killers.*

Get on the bus.
Don't forget your marching shoes.

Lisa Markley is a singer-songwriter, jazz musician, and teaching artist exiled in Texas. When not torturing young children at the piano, she makes hats which are carried in galleries around the country. More on Lisa's music and touring schedule can be found at lisamarkly.com

Ashley Miranda

sink yr fangs into the shadows that keep me company

my great grandmother passed in october of 2016
from her begat
strong
latina
women

who had suffered
in poverty
and overworked
their way into American culture

cleaning at first
laboring at first

strong women who had been accosted by men
and lived
to resist and speak out against
a man who wishes to accost an entire nation

these women paint my memories
working hard
working solo but with the hands of their sisters and mothers

hands that toil and raise
raise enough to see their own daughters and sons
be more

even though a man accosts and jostles a nation
and incites white (wo)men to devalue latin daughters and sons

the women of my family carry my hands now

i won't be yr citizen of compliance
i will toil and overwork myself, like my mother did,
        like her mother did
to bring my children/my nation
and to raise it to be and have more

than what the world thinks it deserves

how i feel in twenty seventeen

there is a tick inside my mouth
and it's violating my eye space

rape culture just
became the 45th president
of the united states

when i die,
perhaps i'll be born again as a 28-day BC pack
so i can prevent suffering from rape culture

rape culture is blazing on tv
giving the state of the union

rape culture has a name on
a building
in my city
i must pass it to work

rape culture has a space in my brain where it pulls neurons and makes me
flutter not in the manic pixie way, no flutter in an uncontrollable shaking
and breaking down with tears and snot and shaking a memory back into
my body

rape culture is designing a nation
letting boys be boys be rape

letting sitting presidents be rapists
be racists letting them take from us
always taking from our bodies

and i'm sitting on a train, looking at rape culture, sitting high
and i'm shaking
and shaking
and shaking

Ashley Miranda is a latinx poet from Chicago. Her work has been or will be featured in the Denver Quarterly, Lockjaw Magazine, CCM's "A Shadow Map," and other publications. She spends a lot of time calling out the sitting president on twitter @dustwhispers.

Running From The Pumpkin King

We leave with as much money as we can steal from ourselves. The highest amount the ATM will dispense in a day. I've saved but it's not enough; there's never enough. But bills aren't due for another week and that next line on the calendar seems so very far away, like maybe we could stop right here and refuse to budge, frozen on the first Thursday of October when we can still cackle and carve leering grins into a gourd's flesh and sleep knowing the worst is only yet to come but not here. Not yet.

We leave Portland before dawn and watch the sun rise over the nothingness where Oregon slips into Nevada without a witness. A shuttle whisks us from the terminal to our hotel that is new but not really—bones of a vintage casino rehauled, costing investors hundreds of millions of dollars. The Las Vegas Strip sheds and implodes and guts itself like a rolling tide, drawing the landscape new each year.

My luggage sags with falsehoods: fake eyelashes, Spanx, costume jewelry. I leave my husband Matt at a machine where our finances will be decided by a dancing lobster in sunglasses. I pass girls in pasties painted as American flags and women in ORGASM CLINIC t-shirts, beyond a lake with a depth only reaching my ankles and into the Bellagio's gardens. They had shipped in the same giant pumpkins they grew in my rural Oregon town and arranged the exotic gourds in a cornucopia the size of Matt's Toyota Tundra. Asian tourists lower their phones and brush their fingers against the waxy orange skins as if searching for a pulse, a sign that they are nudging something real. The pumpkins are true but they are terrified. As sad as the lettuce in Portland after Christmas, still dreaming of Mexico and accepting its inevitable rain-soaked death.

In the salon a man teases my baby-fine hair into an enormous bouffant I don't dare touch, for fear it will disintegrate like cotton candy. Next door at Caesars Palace, another man paints my eyes with winged Cleopatra liner. It takes him thirty minutes to get it just right, each stroke a deeper disguise. I arrange my face in an optimistic smile as he tells me about his long-distance relationship with someone in Tunisia. These men talk about music and wearing what you love and fucking haters and who their cousin the Uber Black driver has picked up between Hakkasan and XS nightclubs. This contrived world of joy and beauty and pleasure seems untouchable. None of us mention who we're voting for and how terrified we are of the incorrect answer because the decision is obvious. We elect for this never to end.

I leave the Forum Shops at Caesar's with the same MAC makeup bag they hand out at the mall I visit back home, but this mall is painted gold with casts of naked gods and goddesses emerging from cerulean fountains and a three-story spiral escalator twisting up to a fresco sky. At Venus's feet, an old man naps on his shoulders, a Panda Express cup waiting to catch falling pennies. The value of one Fendi purse in the windows above him would house him for a month, maybe two in something small and away. What is more vulgar, I think, than carrying around a bag worth as much as someone's shelter?

My fluffed hair and black eyes would feed him for a week. I am just as disgusting as the dancing fountains as California's orchards die of thirst, the buffet plates piled and abandoned, the million lights drowning out the stars.

The implosion is as inevitable as it is beautiful.

It creeps through in the dumpsters and parking garages behind the casino's perfect front doors. It wafts up from the sidewalk confetti of escort calling cards and rapture pamphlets; when you get a little too close to a woman in skyscraper stilettos and a sequined dress, and can trace the bags under eyes that have barely seen two decades around the sun, a falling sensation as you realize that the city is a vampire and you're only here for a couple of short days in a whole life outside of its bubble.

But unlike in that real world, there are ten thousand ways to forget. I duck into a cocktail bar disguised as a smoothie shop. They add an extra shot of Patron to my cucumber mint infusion.

"On the house, gorgeous," he says. He slides me a punch card to earn one free, like every other day and my bitter, burnt coffee.

★

A few weeks before Vegas I was in Seattle visiting an old friend. The naked, micro-penis Donald Trump statue had just landed on Capitol Hill. It was still September and there was time. You could register, you could get a passport. Maybe we could all be better.

"Do you have to come back up here for the holidays?" He asked after we'd finished shots.

"I think so, but Christmas is going to be weird this year, so close to the wedding and everything." My sister was getting married in January. People were still marching forward, making plans for 2017 as if seasons would keep unspooling. Like life went on. "We're all going to be broke and I don't have any time off." I was using it all up on vacations. Glacier National Park, Disneyland, Las Vegas. Two thousand sixteen would be a contender for best year of my life if I weren't so panicked it would be my last.

"But you'll all be on the same page at least," he said.

"Yeah." The liquor slicked my tongue just enough to let loose what I knew better than to speak. "I've been thinking about the holidays and how special I want it to be, like get out all my decorations and bake all my favorite cookies and just try my best, you know? Because maybe it's going to be the last one we have."

"Jesus, you're scaring me."

I apologized. I should know better.

We eat at a Chinese restaurant designed to make you feel like you're inside a fish bowl, framed in goldfish tanks and carved white wave ceilings. I remember it from the first time I was in Vegas as a teenager, at the mercy of parents trying their best to make a memorable summer vacation within budget. It was as impossible for me to get into as the DJ-side table at TAO was for me now; expensive food that no one else in my family wanted to eat.

"Let's try this place," I told Matt, feeling one of those rare jolts of adulthood joy that no one can tell you where the fuck you can and can't have lunch, or pressure you not to order a soda, or that appetizers are off-limits.

We order pork soup dumplings that arrive in a bamboo steamer. A woman with a convention lanyard watches us fan the magma-hot pillows from her next-door table, which is wedged closer to ours than necessary. "Have you been here before?" she strikes up a conversation. She asks if we have kids, and I guffaw. The laughter ricochets off the tanks, louder than I intended, like when I answer someone with my headphones on. I want to ask her how I could possibly send anything I love out into this husk of a world. I want to tell her about how whenever I read about the impending doom of avocadoes or coastal cities or reindeer or aboriginal fishing villages I take their rough estimate year of doom and count back how old I will be, and feel relief flood through my nerves when I realize that I'll most definitely be dead. I want to know if anyone else in history has daydreamed on the promise of the future and rejoiced mortality.

I ask if she's planning to see any shows.

★

We walk until our feet feel like hamburger. There are no idle moments to scroll through Twitter. None of the bars or restaurants are playing the news. I only hop on my phone long enough to post pictures. Pretending to be squashed by the two-story flamingo statue, a selfie with Gordon Ramsay, a steak that cost almost as much as our hotel room. The Instagrams are framed by cryptic missives from my friends.

Is this real life?

TFW you see the GOP hit the iceberg.

I wonder if it is possible, that I can leave Oregon after months of banning myself from the evening news and *The New York Times* thinkpieces because I feel like my heart is going to stop, I can come home to a resolution? Escapism works?

While I order hard root beer and feed the last of our twenties into a machine that eats it up and spits out spins, the Pussygate memes are launching. The 140 characters seem so optimistic, as if everyone I know is glimpsing light. It's easy to forget that nothing, not one single heinous, irreversibly disgusting thing this monster has said or done or promised, has lingered longer than a daily paper run. Not while it's knitted into the fear. Not when the alternative is a woman.

We walk to the end of the strip, further than I've ever been before. The resorts and shopping palaces level into vacant lots and abandoned projects. Trump Tower stands alone, glistening gold like the tinfoil in *Charlie and the Chocolate Factory*'s ticket. I snap a picture of my left hand flipping it off and upload it onto Facebook and Twitter.

Thank you! My friends say. It feels just as powerful as my vote; as worthless as my dread.

★

When I was a kid in history class, I used to play Would I Kill Myself? Europe in World War II was Yes. The Revolutionary War was No. The Great Depression was a Maybe. The theoretical nuclear annihilation my 8th grade teacher made us watch in *The Day After* was the most rousing ABSOLUTELY. It was all a dialogue in my head; I just assumed everyone else was asking the same question.

It's not that I wanted to die. A Yes sank me; the knowledge that I'd rather end than endure the suffering and witness the cruelty. I was a coward, but at least I knew it. There was comfort in that acceptance—in case of apocalypse, break glass.

Can I live through the end of American government, I ask silently of myself. The jury is out. I wonder when I'll need an answer. Everything has happened so incrementally, this acceptance of white supremacy, xenophobia, totalitarianism, this Pumpkin Hitler. There is no winning, even if I wake up from a Xanax-induced coma on November 9th and my phone screen is filled with soft shades of blue. His legion remains. A flitter with implosion awaits every fourth year from now until my eternity.

★

We wait to leave on the ass-end of the casino. Defeated fans in LA Kings jerseys chain-smoke and wait for Uber rides. A whole SuperShuttle bus loops around to pick up only the two of us to an airport that will be so empty, the TSA takes the time to unpack all the souvenir soaps in my carry-on.

The driver turns away from the lights onto Paradise Road, past a string of mobile unit hiring centers, an abandoned night club and a shuttered auto dealership. The bus TV screen runs down everything we didn't do: Chippendales, indoor skydiving, the Atomic Testing Museum.

"You two voting for Trump?" the driver asks from nowhere.

I slip on my sunglasses even though it's dusk. I don't have the energy to police my expression. "I'd sooner die," I tell him.

"He sure beats the alternative though, ya know?" He continues. "At least you know what you're getting into with a businessman. Not a liar."

I wonder how long I can stretch out the last few hundred dollars in our bank account, if they'd give us a higher credit limit, if we could stay hidden in the blinding shadows of Pleasure Island for the rest of the month. I wonder how long the gold will glisten after this is all over. How much time will pass before the sand carves the glass and cement into phantoms of what we once were.

I turn my headphones on. I wait.

Tabitha Blankenbiller is a graduate of the Pacific University MFA program living outside of Portland, Oregon. Her essays have appeared in a number of journals including The Rumpus, Hobart, Barrelhouse, The Establishment, Brevity, and Passages North. Her debut collection *EATS OF EDEN* is forthcoming from Alternating Current Press.

Jessica Fenlon

she persisted

Almost any domestic abuser
when recounting the event

will state in passing
"I warned her"

[for the way male republicans spoke about Elizabeth Warren after silencing
her when she attempted to read Mrs. King's letter during the Sessions hearings]

Poet & new media artist Jessica Fenlon lives in Milwaukee, WI, USA. Her second book of poetry, *Manual for Wayward Angels*, was published by Pittsburgh's 6 Gallery Press in early 2017. Her artwork has exhibited in Ireland, England, Italy, Bulgaria, Poland, The Netherlands, Germany, Egypt, Cuba, China, and the United States.

For work samples & exhibition history, please visit station–number–six.com.

Anita Olivia Koester

Tapestry with White Columns

It's easy to drown in the mouth of a man.
Sometimes the boat house is pristine
as a white house, it appears safe to enter.
Safety itself is a fraught concept. So is
preservation. Barrel-aged whiskey
and muddled cherries smart the nostrils,
the throats of some men are charred ash-grey
and dry as aged-skulls. Some men's souls
haven't but a shack to bed down in.
Some men's souls scurry like rats
through an elephant graveyard.
Halls of mirrors only obscure the portrait.
Statues of self-crowned kings
are defaced throughout history.
A woman's soul is tusked and trumpeting,
is plump and yellow-crested, filled with
caverns of amethyst, pyrite, and charcoal.
Pyrite isn't fool's gold at all.
The people built cradles with it.
The people line their hearths with it.
It's the other gold, slung crusted in crystals
round the neck and wrist of the woman imprisoned
in please that wearies me. Not all American dreaming
is created equal nor unalienable.
Some dreams can be torn from the heart.
Some dreams are smothered in bed-chambers
others blacklisted, refused entry, interned, deported,
lynched. Some dreams are not self-evident.
Then there are those gluttonous dreamers,
atavistic and cannibalistic, they feed off of fear.
I dreamt of a woman crying out under a hand
over her mouth, saying *no, no, no*, still saying *please*,
and the city of grass moving alongside her,
beneath her, on top of her, carrying the bright
weight of her through the corridors, tunnels,
under the overpass and everyone minding
their business as the skies grew heavy with soot
and the rains stained the pavement red
and the resurrection was a long time coming.

Anita Olivia Koester is a Chicago poet and author of the chapbooks *Marco Polo* (Hermeneutic Chaos Press), *Apples or Pomegranates* forthcoming with Porkbelly Press, and *Arrow Songs* which won Paper Nautilus' Vella Chapbook Contest. Her poems have been nominated for Best New Poets and Pushcart Prizes, and won Midwestern Gothic's Lake Prize, So to Speak's Annual Poetry Contest, as well as the Jo-Anne Hirshfield Memorial Poetry Award. Her poetry is published or forthcoming in Vinyl, CALYX Journal, Tupelo Quarterly, Tahoma Literary Review, Pittsburgh Poetry Review, and elsewhere. Visit her online at anitaoliviakoester.com

Clara Silverstein

Kissing Donald Trump

I'm starstruck, unguarded,
teenage whirligig of curls,
several inches of breasts too profuse.
When we meet, he tugs my skirt
into place; he's three times
my age and a foot taller.
He bends, red faced, "You're beautiful,"
doesn't wait, just kisses me,
moves in very heavily.
Tic Tacs explode in my mouth
like broken teeth.

Clara Silverstein is the Boston-based author of the memoir *White Girl: A Story of School Desegregation* (University of Georgia Press), and three cookbooks. Her poems were chosen for display at Boston City Hall and have been published in journals including Blackbird, and the Paterson Literary Review. Her website is clarasilverstein.com

Kelly Grace Thomas

In the Locker Room with Your President

She, in fact, wanted to get out. But
the star can do anything
to her
too heavily and everything.
Move, bitch.
Furniture show. Grab'em by the pussy
just in case they don't wait. Grab
anything. Tic Tacs. Sudden tits.
Don't even, bitch.
Better magnet just in case.
Kiss: wanted.
Bitch grab: wanted
Get there. I moved her phony. You can.
Grab'em big. Don't wait.
Pussy, tits and everything. She's magnet.
Couldn't move. She couldn't.
The pussy is nice furniture.
Move on it. On her. I moved the furniture.
And when you're a star,
don't wait. Even when they bitch, I just start.
Anything pussy
you do. I took her
shopping bitch couldn't marry.
Automatically changed her
furniture now.
I don't even wait. I don't even wait.

Kelly Grace Thomas is the winner of the 2017 Neil Postman Award for Metaphor from Rattle and a two-time Pushcart Prize nominee. *BOAT/ BURNED*, her first full-length collection, is forthcoming from YesYes Books. Kelly's poems have appeared or are forthcoming in: DIAGRAM, Tinderbox, Nashville Review, Sixth Finch, Muzzle, PANK and more. Kelly was also a 2016 Fellow for the Kenyon Review Young Writers Workshop. Kelly works to bring poetry to underserved youth as the Manager of Education and Pedagogy for Get Lit-Words Ignite. She is also the co-author of Words Ignite: Explore, Write and Perform, Classic and Spoken Word Poetry (Literary Riot). She lives in Los Angeles and is working on her first novel Only 10,001. For more of her work, visit kellygracethomas.com

Meghan O'Hern

When Hate Wins

on the night hate wins
before even turning off the tv
my roommate tells me
"at least you can still move to canada"
as if this country is not mine too

my brother calls me at 1:43 a.m.
                        just to make sure i am still alive

the next day a nightmare incarnate
the shirt i wear reads, "gay ok"
and i lose track of how many people tell me i am brave
my existence—a political statement
a chorus of "everything will be okay"
i'm supposed to move on
swallow this

at the peaceful protest
someone casually mentions
our future leader is awaiting trial for rape
his supporters—no longer faceless hatred
but the boy who took my silence as a yes

walking the two blocks home alone
"fucking dyke"
a man spits in my direction
and i don't want to
but i freeze
watch him drive away
over my shoulder
                        breathe

                                                walk
my roommate says
"well it's not like you were hiding it"

everything in me hollows
this is our home. not his. ours.
so i lock myself in my room
realize it's too much like a closet

Meghan O'Hern received her B.A. in English and Creative Writing from Bradley University in Peoria, IL. Her work centers on equality, sexuality, and disability. Her first book, *Rising from the Ashes*, is available now from Weasel Press.

On Pork & Politics In County Baldwin, The Long & Short Of It When A Tower Is Not A Fine Hotel Or A Resort But A Sausage Festival Cum Political Rally Before A National Election

(You have all the characteristics of a popular politician: a horrible voice,
bad breeding, and a vulgar manner. —- Aristophanes, c 424 BC)

Orange and red = Orangeade = fossil fuel = seeing red. She has a blister
on her lip. Underneath the scab, it is red. The scab hides redness. On a
rut-red road when the sun raises its fist, she can be heard in the heart
of Elberta singing:

> *Orange is the color of my suitor's hair, his face he claims is wondrous, fair,*
> *his wandering eyes and curious hands.*
> *He loves the ground on which I stand. He loves the ground on which I stand.*
> *Orange is the color of my suitor's hair.*

But... But... what difference does color make in that box of Crayola Crayon
Colors:
"Burnt Orange," "Mango Tango," "Atomic Tangerine," "Radical Red,"—
also Black,
and that is the question: To mark in the box or not to? In November, the
mark was black, not red. It is called a vote – not a popular vote but electoral. It
refers to community, to a red town in a red state with a sausage festival where
trumpets blared and the

> Rostbratwurst made from finely minced pork and beef; serve on bun.
> Blood Sausage made with congealed pig blood; slice and eat cold.
> Knockwurst can be pickled, but best when smoked.
> Leberkase which is similar to pink meatloaf

there where 7,000 pounds of sausage are sold each year—there where 30,000
folks, most with red necks, feast on organ meat, on red beans, cabbage, some
on sugardaddies.

The Festival, near the intersection of Main Street and State
lies across from the Town Hall which is a stone's throw,
more or less, from the Water Tower. No pets, but anybody
can be denied entry without real explanation.

The pigs in their pens, in their parlors, are slopped once a day,
as they await hog heaven. The craft booths are 10 feet by 10 feet.

Adriana Maybelle Annie met her Don as near as the hand, the wrist,
his skiff on the 41.3 mile River Styx in southwestern Alabama—
(Charon drunk as a coot on Jim beam. Nevermind) tied to the dock.
It was on board he drawled, "Ba- by," "Sugar-doll," "Lil' Punkin',"
took her below deck to make hay. He did not know she was a tease,
one hard-to-get *Magna cum laude* from the Polytechnic Institute
now called Auburn.

She knew the difference, bless her heart, between lie and lay,
and often downed dirty martinis with her supper—two at most.
Her mama told her to be careful of what she put in her mouth.

She shunned men with small accoutrements and was not Nobodaddy's
porn-pussy. She'd majored in English, studied John Cage, James Joyce:
Whether these be sins or virtues old nobodaddy will tell us at doomsday leet.
She'd read Aristophanes' play, *The Knight* about a sausage vendor elected leader
and about Shakespeare's fat Falstaff. Uninviting men would not tickle her
catastrophe—

NoNoNoNoNo, not at this market, *NoNoNoNo.*

Really now, that rodomontade, that empty, boasting, blustering,
trumpeting rogue who would grab a rapallion with his own hungry hands!
Hands that merrily knead. Doesn't he know that one ass is not the same
as another,
the blow-hard?

Still chopping onions made her cry.

"I'm coming," he called, heading toward the ship's galley
where she was stirring gumbo full of shrimp and crab.
He was after her badonkadonk. She thought he was telling
of the Lord, her eyes bleary with tears. Hard to see straight.
She thought he was Jesus resurrected from the dead, but
pausing in the process of her thinking, she realized it was
Parousia. Truly. The Second Coming.

An announcement came then, loud like a trumpet call,
sound harking over the speaker, sound like pigs squealing:
Time for the Weiner 5K Walk and the 1 Mile Fun Run.
She came then, came to her senses at the word, "FUN,"
her page-boy hair combed down, unfrizzed. She bit her lip
until it bled and lickety-split, took off running.

Sue B. Walker is a retired English professor, the publisher of Negative Capability Press, and Poet Laureate of Alabama from 2003-2012.

january 20, 2017

today, i woke up in an america afraid to speak its own name. a nation so distressed it had mother nature wailing. a country knee deep in apologies and falsities. a year ago, i was sitting in an ap u.s. history class learning about the men that had built our cities on buried backs of others. a class taught by a woman, about men. a curriculum normalizing the way things have always been. a year ago, i was more concerned with the way my report card looked than how i would speak up for myself tomorrow. a year ago, i used the word "feminist" to describe my sister, not myself. a year ago, i sat patiently in the closet, keeping my mouth shut and head down. a year ago, i was sure that today would not happen and yet, this morning i woke up. ate breakfast. got dressed. brushed my teeth.

the past year has not been one without challenge. there have been few days i've woken up and not had to force feed myself courage. but maturity does not come without growing pains just like justice does not come without speaking up. this fight is far from over. that is not to say that there will not be days it is hard to get up or that my feminism will be safer inside, but i have grown tired of waiting for things to work out the way i want them to. this year has been one of grief. but despair will fade, and in its place we will stand. and we will march. and i will continue to grow.

Amelia Newett is an eighteen-year-old student at Johns Hopkins University in Baltimore, MD. Over the past few years, she has taken numerous creative writing courses both in and out of school. She taught creative writing, with an emphasis on poetry, at camps for young children for three summers during high school. She participated in poetry slams (leading her team to both a second and, the following year, a first place ranking in the county), and became a part of the widely known Get Lit Players. With the GLPs she has traveled across Los Angeles County to perform at high schools, encourage others to participate, and explain how poetry has shaped her life.

to the full professor who told me, a teaching assistant, to grow a thicker skin after the inauguration

you are telling
me my skin
is gossamer—that
i must weave
steel around myself, must
temper it, must
cradle those
who say *they*
let too much through
their skin—but i am
they. my family, my history,
written in dark ink on my
skin, my thin skin, my
weak skin, my brown paper
skin, my skin already exposed,
always exposed, my neck
bare for you. my armor is
what it is, is silk, is stronger
than it appears, but what you ask,
is too much, too much—i cannot, do not
want to build more walls.

Anna Cabe is an MFA candidate in fiction at Indiana University and the nonfiction editor of Indiana Review. Her work has appeared or is forthcoming in Bitch, The Toast, SmokeLong Quarterly, Joyland, Vol. 1 Brooklyn, Cleaver, Expanded Horizons, and Noble/Gas Qtrly, among others. She was a 2015 Kore Press Short Fiction Award semifinalist, a finalist for Midwestern Gothic's Summer 2016 Flash Fiction Series, and a finalist for the 2015 Boulevard Short Fiction Contest for Emerging Writers. You can find Anna at annacabe.com.

American Carnage

Like a ruby sun
setting in July
or apple peel
caught in between
my two closest
teeth, we anticipate
how all we
know will change
and yes, that
sounds dramatic and
yes, it is
necessary. Have you
been listening/have
you noticed the
way people say
"be safe" nowadays,
as if we
can't be whispering
those words to
ourselves enough. Be
safe. Be safe.
Be safe. Be
safe. Be safe.
Be. Be. Be.
Safe. Safe. Safe.
I am holding
my palms out,
one for accepting
and one for
offering. Give me
your words, your
concerns, your doubts,
your breath. Give
me everything I
can't keep in
my pockets. I'll
offer you this:
A memory of
days before we
were afraid, before

we left with
saying, "be safe"
to head out
to the grocery
store. Before our
fear of crowds,
before our empty
pockets, empty palms,
empty motives, except
for the ability
to repeat to
others as well
as ourselves, "these
hands." Please, help
yourself. I never
wanted to live
in my parents'
world. But here
I am. Watching.
My years turning
the crank—watching
as the Jack
leans closer until
I can feel.
His hot breath.
Fingering. Down
my neck.

Lisa Folkmire is an MFA in writing candidate at Vermont College of Fine Arts with an emphasis in poetry. Her work has been previously published in Heron Tree Literary Arts Journal, Yellow Chair Review, Erstwhile Magazine, Atlas and Alice, among others.

WHO CONTROLS THE PAST CONTROLS THE FUTURE
—George Orwell, *1984*

Ghazal: A Night Already Devoid of Stars

> *Returning violence for violence multiplies violence,*
> *adding a deeper darkness to a night already devoid*
> *of stars*—Martin Luther King Jr.

The stars seem dimmer, further away tonight,
the TV finally turned off, the night

moving across the globe, lights going out
in a wave. I wait on my balcony. Tonight's

forecast: meteor showers. The sky drains
of light. A dying star shoots across night's

dark screen. Moments ago, a lighted stage,
applause for a man who claimed the night

for himself, promised to keep us safe,
pledged to return violence, multiply night

in the foreign places it hides, all darkness
walled out. But it was hiding in plain sight tonight.

Hate can't drive out hate, Martin Luther King
said. *Only love can do that.* And tonight

I'm remembering something I read once,
that our blood comes from dying stars. Yes, night

is mingled with the starlight, but we can
be the starlight or we can be the night.

Today, another bombing in return
for last week's bombing. Fear is like moonless night.

It obscures everything, makes us lose sight
of truth, conscience, rationale. Yes, the night

is upon us. *It will get worse before*
it gets better, my husband said last night

after the news: severe flooding, more lives
lost, and still the wildfires burn tonight—

I asked him *When?* The round moon looked down
the way I looked at our daughter tonight,

bent to kiss her forehead, switched off the lamp,
the glow-in-the-dark stars lighting her night,

and she called me my favorite name. *Night, night,
Mommy,* she said as I made a wish. *Night, night.*

Jackleen Holton Hookway's poems have been published in The Giant Book of Poetry, and Steve Kowit: This Unspeakably Marvelous Life, and have appeared in Atlanta Review, Bellingham Review, North American Review, Poet Lore, Rattle, and others.

Dubious Declarations

The Donald let us know he hates anti-Semitic threats.
Horrible and *painful* he informed the press,
reading word-for-word from a script
nervous handlers hoped he wouldn't shred
in a pique of unintended honesty
wrapped in truthful hyperbole.
Days earlier he ad-libbed:
I'm the least anti-Semitic person that you've ever seen...
Strong words? Fer sure.
Definitive words? Definitely.
Words as hollow as a plump pumpkin on Halloween?
You betcha.
But where were his words
when Jewish tombstones toppled like styrofoam bowling pins?
when asked what *he* would do to deter bomb threats
      to Jewish community centers?
when his International Holocaust Remembrance Day statement
      neglected to mention Jews?
This Jewish skeptic isn't buying it: Donald's professed
empathy for Jewish culture, community.
Not a dollar's worth.
Not a dime's worth.
Not a penny's worth.
A grandfather of three Jewish children
shouldn't need a script to express revulsion
      for the rise in anti-Semitic acts—
      a rise coincident with his success in the political arena
shouldn't enlist a chief strategist
      who's fostered pro-Nazi meme makers.
His declared abhorrence of anti-Semitism
is just more of the bloviating and blather
that helped to propel him to his current gilded loft.
But the silence of his indifference
is what echoes most loudly
from this "so-called" president.

Rick Blum has been chronicling life's vagaries through essays and poetry for more than 25 years during stints as a nightclub owner, high-tech manager, market research mogul, and, most recently, old geezer. His writings have appeared in Boston Literary Magazine, Thought Notebook Journal, and The Satirist, among others. He is also a frequent contributor to the Humor Times, and has been published in numerous poetry anthologies. Mr. Blum's poem, *The Inertia of Permanence*, was awarded first place in the 2014 Carlisle Poetry Contest. His poem, *Tomfoolery*, received an honorable mention in The Boston Globe Deflategate poetry challenge.

Betsy Sholl

Fifty-Seven Sunflowers In A Lot Between Houses

The wonder of them all September, those bright faces, each on its one leg,
clustered by the sidewalk, a little village, tableau vivant.

Then by late October: prisoners at the gate, gaunt, barely standing
when the liberators arrive, or that big wind off the North Atlantic,

tossing back each stalk like a blast of sound from an invisible speaker,
gust of Shostakovitch chastising Stalin,

his lust for Soviet fields, for grinding flowers down to oil—
flowers that can't live forever bright

on a museum wall, petals thick as the day they were daubed
on canvas—amber, ochre, mustard.

No, these are the dying ones, whose petals turn stringy, then drop,
leaving just spiky sepals.

Once they stood, the whole town, come to greet a hero
struggling his crutches out of the car.

Come November, they slump, citizens before the mass grave
a farmer's unearthed with his plow, heads bowed

over how much they have seen and yet did little.
Or did much without seeing at all.

Betsy Sholl served as Poet Laureate of Maine from 2006 to 2011. Her eighth collection of poetry, *Otherwise Unseeable* (University of Wisconsin), won the 2015 Maine Literary Award for poetry. Other awards include the AWP Prize for Poetry, the Felix Pollak Prize, a National Endowment for the Arts Fellowship, and Maine Individual Artists Grants. She currently teaches in the MFA Program of Vermont College of Fine Arts, and lives in Portland.

The Set Up

These are the days of shift and shape
Where facts are obfuscated by fiction
Where popularity prides itself over principles
And a world of knowledge gives way to a
World of wealth and stupidity
These are the days of deception
Where suited hucksters,
with sun sprayed smiles
trade tall stories and cook up crimes

These are the days of deflection
Where internet stars and celebrities
dictate the news agenda for weeks and weeks
Where tabloid tales and leaked sex tapes
Can make you the President of the USA!

These are the days of ignorance
Big smiles for nabbing a smart phone,
A pat on the back for acquiring new hi-tops,
or a luxury time piece,
clocking wasted minutes
at sonic speed

These are the days of food banks
And meth addicted grandmas
Steel hanger abortions
And click and bait money scams

These are the days of the debt slave
Where you buy buy buy shopping for nothing
'till the day you die,
Where everything's out of reach
A dead end—a stop sign—a one way street.

Saira Viola: Acclaimed poet and author. Twice nominated for Best of The Net Poetry 2017. Her work has appeared in journals and anthologies worldwide. Most notably her poem *Flowers of War* features in The Stop The War Coalition UK. Viola skewers the pieties of the day with her sharp eye for hypocrisy in an age of greed and fantastic wealth, selfie cultivation and mindless mass culture.

Her fiction can be found in her books, *Jukebox* and *Crack Apple and Pop*.

Her poetry collections include: *Flowers of War, Don't Shoot The Messenger, Mini Rebel Chap Book*, and *Fast Food and Gin on The Lawn*.

Gary Shteyngart

Living in Trump's Soviet Union

I grew up in a dystopia—will I have to die in one, too?

When my parents lived in the Soviet Union, having a Jewish-looking physiognomy," as it was called, proved a daily liability. Standing in line for eggs or milk or ham, one could feel the gaze of the shopkeeper running down one's nose, along with the implied suggestion "Why don't you move to Israel already?"

Social media in the era of Trump is essentially Leningrad, 1979. Trump supporters on Twitter have often pointed out my Jewishness. "You look ethnic" was one of the kinder remarks, along with the usual litany of lampshade drawings, oven photos, the "Arbeit Macht Frei" gate at Auschwitz, and other stock Holocaust tropes. It is impossible to know if the person pointing out your ethnicity and telling you to jump into an oven is an amateur troll in St. Petersburg, Florida, or a professional troll in St. Petersburg, Russia. What this election has proved is just how intertwined those two trolls may be.

"Russia will rise from her knees!" Those were the lyrics I heard outside a suburban train station in St. Petersburg half a decade ago. The song was coming out of an ancient tape player next to a bedraggled old woman selling sunflower seeds out of a cup. She examined my physiognomy with a sneer. At the time, this seemed like just a typical Russian scene, the nation's poorest citizens bristling at their humiliation after losing the Cold War, their ire concentrated on a familiar target, the country's dwindling population of Jews. The surprise of 2016—post-Brexit, post-Trump—is just how ably the Russians weaponize those lyrics, tweak them to "Whites will rise from their knees!" and megaphone them into so many ready ears in Eastern and Western Europe and, eventually, onto our own shores. The graffito "Russia is for the Russians," scribbled next to a synagogue, and the words "Vote Trump," written on a torched black church in Mississippi, are separated by the cold waters of the Atlantic but united by an imaginary grievance—a vigil for better times that may never have existed.

I can understand these people. Growing up in nineteen-eighties Queens, my friends and I, as young Russian immigrants, unfamiliar with the language, our parents working menial jobs, looked down on blacks and Latinos, who were portrayed as threats by the Reagan Administration and its local proxies. The first politicized term I learned in America was "welfare queen," even as my own grandmother collected food stamps and received regular shipments of orange government cheese. We hated minorities, even though the neighborhoods many of us lived in were devoid of them. I didn't attend public school, because my parents had seen one black kid on the playground of the excellent school I was zoned for, and so sent me to a wretched parochial school instead. There was an apocryphal story going around our community about a poor Russian boy beaten so badly by a black public-school kid that his mother killed herself.

If Ronald Reagan was the distant protector of us endangered white kids, then Donald Trump was a local pasha. My buddies and I walked past his family's becolumned mansion, in Jamaica Estates, with a sense of awe. Donald was a straight shooter, a magnate, a playboy, a marrier of Eastern European blondes, a conqueror of distant Manhattan. He was everything a teen-ager in Queens could dream of being. If we were ever blessed to meet him, we knew he would understand the racism in our hearts, and we his. Successful people like him made us secure in our own sense of whiteness.

Thirty years later, every Jew on Twitter who has received a Photoshopped version of herself or himself in a concentration-camp outfit followed by "#MAGA" knows how fleeting that sense of security can be. The idea that Jews should move to their "own" country, Israel, brings together racial purists from Nashville to Novosibirsk. The jump from Twitter racism to a black church set aflame on a warm Southern night is steady and predictable. Putin's team has discovered that racism, misogyny, and anti-Semitism bind people closer than any other experiences. These carefully calibrated messages travel from Cyrillic and English keyboards to Breitbart ears and Trump's mouth, sometimes in the space of hours. The message is clear. People want to rise from their knees. Even those who weren't kneeling in the first place.

My parents and grandparents never fully recovered from the strains of having lived in an authoritarian society. Daily compromise ground them down, even after they came to America. They left Russia, but Russia never left them. How do you read through a newspaper composed solely of lies? How do you walk into a store while being Jewish? How do you tell the truth to your children? How do you even know what the truth is? A few days ago, I visited a local public school. On a second-grade civics bulletin board I saw written in large letters: "Citizens have rights—things that you deserve; RESPONSIBILITIES—things you are expected to do; RULES—things you have to follow." The message seemed to have come from a different era. What did those words have to do with America in 2016? I reflexively checked FiveThirtyEight on my phone. I thought, I grew up in a dystopia—will I have to die in one, too?

Gary Shteyngart was born in Leningrad in 1972 and came to the United States seven years later. His most recent book was the memoir *LITTLE FAILURE,* a national bestseller, a finalist for the National Book Critics Circle Award, and chosen by the New York Times as a Notable Book of the Year. His novels include *SUPER SAD TRUE LOVE STORY, ABSURDISTAN,* and *THE RUSSIAN DEBUTANTE'S HANDBOOK.* His books have been translated into twenty-nine languages. Shteyngart lives in New York City.

2020

My lover Mohammed and I had joined
husband to husband in Niagara Falls
six years before but after our right
to marry was nullified I removed my
mother's miraculous medal from around
my neck and signed up for the Registry
together with Mohammed so of course
we couldn't vote yesterday but at least
we had a home in which to watch Wolf
project the President had lost. Mohammed
and I embraced but within the hour the
tweets began—FALSE, FAKE NEWS,
RIGGED—we saw the army move in
on CNN and the times I see
now will never be the same.

A native New Yorker, James Penha has lived for the past quarter-century in Indonesia. Nominated for Pushcart Prizes in fiction and poetry, his LGBT speculative story, *Leaves,* was a finalist for the Saints and Sinners Short Fiction Contest and so appears in the Saint & Sinners Literary Festival 2017 anthology. His essay, *It's Been a Long Time Coming,* was featured in The New York Times "Modern Love" column in April 2016. Penha edits TheNewVerse.News, an online journal of current-events poetry. Twitter @JamesPenha

An Old Testament

My grandmother lived this.
A more swift version.
There were special police,
dirty mattresses, not
enough food to feed
their indentured camp
living day to day
in the cold forest of Siberia.
We're not there, yet.
This will be a slower burn.
How greedy some men can be.
Is this what God meant
by Noah's flood?
Please, take us two by two.

A South Florida native, Britney Lipton now lives and works in Chicago, where she received her Masters of Fine Arts Writing from The School of the Art Institute of Chicago in 2013. She works for the encyclopedia and writes in her spare time.

Something Dark Beyond Words

There is something waiting in the autumn woods
there ahead right there beyond that crest that hollow
where shadows blend its red claws into the leaves.
You can smell it... something musky on the air
and it beats its massive paws up and down, a trumpeting
and tramping wholly out of place along this casual path,
but it waits for no one and it waits for anyone and
its roaring shakes the earth beneath your feet
and its drumming haunts the dreams of better men
and its drumming wakes its neighbors who start to sing
and they sing of blood and feathers and they sing
of armies trudging forward and they sing of earth
claiming what the seasons bring it out of time
and it's right there up ahead where the crest is
and you can smell it in the air and taste it on your tongue
and revulsion comes to claim you, pulls you back
from that path along the river where the leaves are turning
colors and you shrink into the shadows but it drags you
from your soul and it pulls out all your words and drips
them in the river scattered by the seasons and you
wish for better men and better women but they cry
and run when they see you on that path by the river
there is something in the woods and it is coming it is
no longer waiting in the pages of past history it is
darkness for the country and will burn out our tomorrows
and we have no trumpet to blow down its walls and fences
that were whispers in the wind not so very long ago.

Jared Smith has been a leading voice in the independent press and resistance for more than half a century. The author of 14 volumes of poetry, his work has appeared in hundreds of journals and anthologies in this country, Mexico, Canada, the U.K., France, China, and Taiwan. He has served on the editorial boards of many of the leading literary journals in this country, including The New York Quarterly, Home Planet News, The Pedestal Magazine, and Turtle Island Quarterly.

The Chief Executive

The chief executive retreats to the board room on the top floor of his tower. He sits, his face pale and saggy like skin on a raw chicken breast, looking down at the smart phone he clutches in his trembling hands.

He is awaiting his judgment.

Seeing nothing on screen he wants to see, he pockets the phone. Then, using the smoldering stump of the cigar clenched between his graying teeth, he lights another. He grinds the spent butt into the green marble of the conference table.

The chief executive is not used to waiting.

He takes out his phone and taps a message onto it:

"Mere hrs til I'm in charge again. Will order execution of EVERYONE in yr puny rigged mongrel revolt. U WILL NOT WIN"

The chief executive swivels his Italian leather chair toward a wall of floor-to-ceiling windows. Outside: a breathtaking view of the city at night from ninety stories up. But tonight instead of looking down at neighboring skyscrapers and the ribbons of highway crisscrossing the city below, the chief executive's gaze is drawn upward.

His eyes scan the overcast sky. From the charcoal clouds he expects to see something pitiless emerge and descend. He sees nothing.

He paces across the boardroom, past potted palm trees, a fully stocked wet bar, and pauses at the 78-inch TV screen.

Someone from the new government is on the screen. A woman. He is unable to determine her ethnicity and this irks him. She is muted. He doesn't want to hear her.

She could be saying she's trying to save his life.

She could be saying she intends to let him die.

He turns from her and continues to the opposite window. He looks up.

The sky refuses to betray the machine stalking him from above.

He pouts.

"Resistance. More like reSISSYstance," he taps. "Dirty losers mongrel sissys & ladies cant run a GREAT country. REAL AMERICANS dont follow dirty mongrel sissy ladies."

The chief executive paces back to his Italian leather chair and slumps down into it. He recalls the incident, it must have been less than two years ago, when the prototype attacked the congressman.

★

The congressman had earmarked the project in the first place, channeling billions to a military contractor.

The factory, the congressman had told reporters, would create jobs.

On a leaked security tape, the world saw the prototype veer toward the congressman, its countless retractable metal centipede legs a blur until it was on top of him and using those legs to bind his ankles and wrists. Then the prototype's mandibles closed around the congressman's neck, forming something like a medieval pillory made of steel. Out from the back of prototype, from between its folded wings, rapidly uncoiled a metal structure that resembled, and served the same function as, an 18th Century guillotine.

An engineer engaged the prototype's emergency shut off, but not before the machine dropped its diagonal blade.

The wriggling congressman squirmed loose in time to save his head, but not his nose.

The military contractor's press release described what had happened as a terrible malfunction. The prototype, the contractor insisted, would pose absolutely no threat to law-abiding Americans. The persons responsible for the malfunction had been fired, their security clearances revoked. The press release went on to say that these negligent employees never again would find work in the military robotics sector.

The controversy surrounding the incident subsided when the recovered congressman testified, with the aid of his new false nose, regarding his steadfast support for the contractor's efforts to develop its "HATER"—Hovering AntiTerror Execution Robot—the very machine responsible for separating his nose from his face. Even inside the congressman's mid-Atlantic district, few noticed that their representative resigned instead of seeking reelection, and fewer still noticed he remained in Washington to become the military contractor's chief lobbyist.

At a private meeting between only the lobbyist with the false nose, the chief executive, and the chief executive's trusted advisor, the chief executive had looked into the pale eyes of this lobbyist and saw a man with whom he could do business. The lobbyist shared classified footage of the automated anti-terror apparatus biting heads off of various gang leaders inside a prison. The trusted advisor grinned, his face like a fat fist squeezing meat between its thick fingers, and gave a nod of approval. That was all the chief executive needed to see to be convinced.

The chief executive, his trusted advisor, and the rest of his board bought stock in the contractor.

Seven months later the chief executive signed a bill allocating federal funds for local police to use HATERs to supplement their forces.

"To jobs," said the lobbyist with the false nose, raising his champagne glass in salute to the party leaders whose reelection campaigns his employer promised to fund.

"To jobs," echoed the chief executive and his board.

The chief executive's trusted advisor briefed the chief executive each week on contractor's steadily climbing stock prices and its HATER output and the stream of executions the machines were carrying out.

"Thanks to innovation, Americans are safe again," the chief executive told a crowd of various elected and unelected lackeys, hangers-on, and minions. "Thanks to innovation, Americans can sleep soundly again."

From the lackeys, hangers-on, and minions: applause.

"Jobs!" he added.

From the lackeys, hangers on, and minions: more applause.

★

Savoring the memory of the applause, the chief executive rummages through his briefcase in the center of the conference table.

The battery in his phone is nearly dead. He's looking for a power cord to plug into the wall and charge it. "Gotcha," he mumbles, catching the tangled black cord between his fingers and pulling it out like an oversized pube.

He plugs his phone in and types:

"traitor SCUM will BEG FOR MERCY! Great Americans dont give in to antiamerican weaklings & whiners, we FIGHT & WIN & WIN until we WIN FOREVER"

★

The chief executive was unaware anything was wrong with the HATERs until the chief executive's trusted advisor brought a technical officer from the contractor to the chief executive's office to deliver a top-secret briefing.

"Something has gone wrong with the HATERs," the technical officer said.

"What has gone wrong with the HATERs?" the chief executive asked.

"Something," repeated the technical officer. "We're not yet sure precisely what."

"Precisely what is wrong," interjected the trusted advisor, "is that in the last forty-eight hours the HATERs have decapitated five lobbyists, eight corporate executives, fourteen members of Congress, nineteen generals, twenty-three corporate lawyers, and at least one cabinet member."

The chief executive rubbed his eyes and aimed them at the technical officer. He already hadn't been sleeping well. "Tell me you're doing something about this," he said. "No. Tell me something has already been done about this."

"The emergency shut off has been engaged," said the technical officer. "The HATERs will be collected. The problem will be isolated."

"So you're telling me there was a crisis," said the chief executive, "but the crisis is over."

"The thing is, we don't know why the HATERs turned on our people," said the trusted advisor through his clenched meat-face. "But the technical officer has a theory."

"What's your theory?"

"We know that right before the HATERs turned, they received an upgrade," said the technical officer. "I'm not 100 percent certain, but my theory is, instead of an upgrade, they received a downgrade. To their original algorithm."

"What the fuck does that mean?" The chief executive was used to not understanding what others are saying, but he was not used to not pretending that he understands.

The trusted advisor puts his hands on the chief executive's shoulders. They locked eyes. "He means the HATERs have devolved back to their original programming. He thinks they are back to the programming that cost that congressman his nose," said the trusted advisor.

"The original programming?"

"The algorithm," corrected the technical officer.

The chief executive struggled to contain his frustration. "What. The fuck. Does that mean?"

"I'm sorry," said the technical officer. "The original algorithm was designed to direct the HATERs simply to target those terrorists who, according to a complex, multifactor analysis, if killed, would result in the greatest number of potential lives saved."

"That sounds great," said the chief executive. "That sounds simple. Eliminate the terrorist leaders first. Cut off the head of the snake. Heads of the snakes. Why is that a problem?"

"The problem is that the original algorithm failed to distinguish terrorists from non-terrorists," said the trusted advisor.

"I still don't understand."

Slowly, the trusted advisor explained so that the chief executive could understand.

"We don't know if it was a just a malfunction," concluded the trusted advisor, "or if it was a hack. But we do know the algorithm's creator is missing, and that he had a nickname for his program."

"Don't tell him the nickname," said the technical officer.

"I have to tell him the nickname," said the trusted advisor.

"Tell me the nickname," ordered the chief executive.

The trusted advisor sighed, shifted awkwardly with his hands in his pants pockets, and did not meet the chief executive's eyes. "He called it the Hitler Killer."

After a long pause, the chief executive said, "And these HATERs, they've all been shut down?"

The technical officer hesitated before answering. "All of the HATERs are accounted for," he said. "All but one. The original, the prototype—the one that took off that congressman's nose—has gone missing."

★

When the executions of business and government leaders came to light, panic ensued.

Even after the other elites received official reassurances that the threat had almost entirely been eliminated, and that the nation's top hackers and military agents were devoted to nothing but bringing down that last rogue robot, almost every powerful person in the U.S. fled or hid.

These were people, after all, who were not used to facing any risk or hazard they had not willfully chosen to face.

Corporate titans were the first to evacuate. Their underlings soon followed. Before long, full-blown panic spread from the private to the public sector. Those in government who had enacted policies that put profits before people followed their campaign donors offshore or begged to join their underground luxury bunkers.

The news-watching public, meanwhile, was soon well aware that their leaders had disappeared. After learning the cause of the ruling corporate and political class' disappearance was its vulnerability to an attack by a robot programmed to kill those who were complicit in millions of deaths, the first celebrations, in retrospect, could seem timid.

The big parties didn't start until after the initial shock of plunging financial markets and shrieking television pundits subsided.

Soon, new people seized power—people whose futures were not tied to the rising fortunes of corporations, people who saw a better future in decoupling society's prosperity from the system that for so long had kept so many others powerless, people who were willing to replace the old order with a new vision.

The people who seized power did so in part because they had no fear that a robot who murders murderers would target them. For all their lives, these people—teachers, nurses, cooks, cleaners, and other workers—had been the carers, the life-savers, the protectors.

★

By the time the chief executive realized almost everyone he'd thought of as an ally had left him behind, it was too late.

Only his trusted advisor remained by his side.

Three weeks into the crisis, the chief executive attempted a show of strength. He and his trusted advisor emerged from the underground chamber at the bottom of the chief executive's tower to hold a press conference. They held the press conference in front of the tower's main entrance, where marble columns detailed with golden leaves and silver swirls framed the chief executive's crystal podium.

News cameras swarmed the chief executive as he raged against the elites who betrayed him, his opponents who usurped him, and the hackers and officers who had failed to eliminate the robot menace.

His trusted advisor stood by his side, grim-faced and radiating an air of quiet determination.

The chief executive was saying something about the people who had taken power in his absence—unsupported insinuations connecting the color of their skin, their gender, and their religion and their "fundamental disloyalty to the dream of America that all true patriots embrace"—when the HATER swooped out from behind a building and in a few fluid motions quietly and cleanly removed the trusted advisor's head.

★

The chief executive sends another message from his charging phone: "robots took YOUR JOBS, AMERICANS. will u let a robot take me too?!"

He is biding his time.

He does not know if the people who took over the government disbanded the team that was supposed to be working on stopping the last HATER or if the team is still on the job.

Four days have passed since the machine executed his trusted advisor.

Surely people who are as dedicated to saving lives as the new administration claims to be would not allow a killer robot to continue to stalk the skies if they could help it.

Surely the death of his trusted advisor is a sign of these usurpers' incompetence, their inability to stop the machine, and not their acquiescence to its mission.

Surely he will be saved, and his rightful position as head of the administration will be restored.

Such certainties sustain the chief executive. All his long life, he has chosen certainty when faced with the unknown, and this moment is no other.

The chief executive has no time for uncertainty.

What he has time for, and what his missives are calculated to guard against, is any sense of gratitude or generosity or kindness or forgiveness or graciousness he might allow himself to feel if this new government succeeds in saving him.

Because if the new government does succeed in saving him, any warm feelings he allows himself will only get in the way when he, as he must, dedicates his remaining days to destroying all they have created.

Rick Claypool is the author of *Leech Girl Lives*, a weird pulp dystopian novel of resistance, coming in 2017 from Spaceboy Books. He lives in Pittsburgh. For more about Rick, visit rickclaypool.org.

President Bannon - February 1
Geoffry Smalley

Olympia

The news has gone so far beyond absurd
that I can't watch it anymore; the little boxes
with their talking heads all talking
about the same damn thing. So I switch
the channel again, let myself be mesmerized
by the swimmers with their exquisite butterfly
wings, the way their bodies undulate
through the water, rising open-mouthed
as if in praise, then diving down, making it seem effortless.
And I'm reminded of Leni Riefenstahl's film *Olympia*,
documenting the 1936 games in Berlin,
and how, as the movie progresses, the athletes, in shadowy
black and white, leave the stadium behind, turn
godlike, their sculpted bodies blossoming
like time-lapse flowers in the sky.
Yesterday, scrolling down my Facebook feed,
I read about a woman in Missouri who saw Donald Trump's
likeness in a tub of butter, the way once-upon-a-time
somebody was always glimpsing the Virgin Mother
in everything. But there it was, the face
I see in every other post, bubbling up in the yellow
spread, bulbous mouth frozen mid-holler.
The swimmers in the individual medley form a graceful V
like a flock of soaring geese, the pool morphing into
Riefenstahl's majestic sky. I have a friend who can see
the spirit animal in everyone. For her, every trip
to the grocery store is a safari. But I understand it now,
watching these swimmers mount their blocks;
this one's a gazelle, that one, a panther.
Leni Riefenstahl loved Hilter. Her beautiful films
were the glorious Aryan face of his regime.
And before the ceremonies began, her camera lingered
on him, his right arm raised to a surging sea of outstretched arms.
Though the mood is festive, her chiaroscuro
montage takes on the somber tones of history.
But today, I love the swimmers for what our animal bodies can do
when the spirit wants it enough. I lean forward as the one
in the middle lane closes in on the world record line.
Someone strung up a confederate flag at a Trump rally
yesterday, which, I told my husband, is exactly what I would do

if I were a protester: I'd disguise myself as an asshat,
hoist it up and wait for the cameras.
But of course that wasn't a joke, either.
Riefenstahl disavowed the Nazis after the war,
but I wonder if her love lived on in some secret bunker
of her heart where she only dreamed in black and white.
Another record is broken, a new medalist stands
on the platform. I can't help it, my eyes well up.
The lady in Missouri says she thought for a moment
about putting her tub of butter on eBay
to see what she could fetch for it, but in the end,
she just wanted buttered toast, so she dipped a knife
in, and handily scraped away the apparition
of that little, angry face.

* Jackleen's bio previously appears on page 70

William Trowbridge

WHITEOUT

In 1845, Rear Admiral Sir John Franklin and a crew
of 124 embarked on a fatal voyage to find the Northwest
Passage. On word of their failure and death, England still
hailed Franklin as a hero of the Empire

For fear of succumbing to the ways
of savages, the officers eschewed

blubber for tinned meats that leaked
lead from the seams, refused parkas,

choosing flannel coats that got soaked,
then froze. They turned their backs

on dogsleds and igloos, which also stank
of "going native"—something their store

of bibles, novels, carpet slippers,
silverware, and button polishers

assuredly did not. Finally, in place
of blubber, protection from the scurvy

that wracked their bones, the still-living—
snow-blind and starving, their ship

bound fast in Arctic ice—gallantly
ate the dead 'til the last survivor froze.

William Trowbridge's seventh poetry collection, *Vanishing Point*, was published by Red Hen Press in April, 2017. His graphic chapbook, *Oldguy: Superhero*, came out from Red Hen in 2016. His other collections are *Put This On, Please: New and Selected Poems*, *Ship of Fool*, *The Complete Book of Kong*, *Flickers*, *O Paradise*, and *Enter Dark Stranger*. He is a faculty mentor in the University of Nebraska Omaha Low-residency MFA in Writing Program and was Poet Laureate of Missouri from 2012 to 2016. For more information, see his website at wiliamtrowbridge.net.

Neeli Cherkovski

Leader of the 'Free' World

the idea of what is
true floats in the mind
of a man whose hands
hold the keys
to mass destruction

but I talk only for my garden's sake,
and when someone writes,
"The leader of the free world
is an amoral piece of crap"
it is just rhetoric and as obvious
as is the sun rising at dawn

I turn to extol the beauty
of the fruit on my lemon tree,
GREEN AND PALE GREEN AND
YELLOW LEMONS, soft or hard, half
hidden in the tangle of branches
or exposed to mantles of mist
breathing down from Twin Peaks

"There is no free world, everything
is bought and paid for," says the monk
who beats a tin drum
in my garden, "Go find a sonnet
and scribe the words... talk of
snails and the black widow spider"

from Finland and Mexico
and Germany I am asked
to send a poem, no one wants
a song to my flowers or a paean
to the lemons, not one word
for the avocado tree or the
tree fern, they want a political
poem, I'm expected
to rant and challenge, to degrade
and affirm the infamy

I love what Yeats wrote,,
"A terrible beauty is born"
on the ridges of our common tongue
and it is splendid to see
how it gains domination
and glows
like ashes from the Auschwitz
death camp
it is as if the people
had been blinded and made to sign
a death warrant

I know why I am reading
a history of the Nazi
death camps, why I turn
Freud into a poet and Kafka
into a sign
for liberation, I am aware
of why I love to splash water
over the beautiful terror
in my garden, the green hose
leaks but it works well enough
here in the free world

                    – March 10, 2017

Neeli Cherkovski recently completed a second installment of papers for his archives at the Bancroft library the University of California Berkeley. His new book, *Elegy for My Beat Generation,* will be published in the fall of 2017.

Jessy Randall

THE OFFENSE

A ten–minute play.

[*Time*]
2017 or later

[*Place*]
Two adjacent interrogation rooms

[*Characters*]
VOICE OF AUTHORITY (VOFA): can be any human
TASHA: a young woman
ZED: a young person

[*TASHA and* ZED *should be roughly the same age. For the play to work, there should be something on the surface causing them difficulty as a couple: perhaps they have different color skin; perhaps one of them is Muslim, or an immigrant; perhaps they are gay; adjust pronouns as necessary.*]

[*Setting*]
The stage is divided by a movable wall, a piece of cardboard will do, with Tasha on one side and Zed on the other. The lights should be able to fade down on one side and up on the other, depending on who's speaking. The idea is that there's one-way glass between the actors and the edge of the stage, so when the actors look toward the audience they see their own reflections. They know, however, that they are being observed. The VOFA can be a person standing in the audience facing the rooms, or a disembodied voice on a PA system.

[LIGHTS *on* BOTH]

ZED. [*stomping feet, yelling*] TASHA! TASHA!

> [*By end of play* ZED *should be hoarse and tired, implying he's kept this up the whole time.*]

> [*TASHA is curled up in corner, shoulders shaking, weeping.*]

[LIGHTS *off for* ZED. LIGHTS *on for* TASHA]

VOFA. State your name, ID number, age, and grade.

[TASHA *attempts to pulls herself together. She can use the "mirror" to tidy herself.*]

VOFA. State your name, ID number, age, and grade.
TASHA. Tasha 3942, 13, Seventh. [*adjust age and grade according to actors, up to "14th grade," i.e., college*]

VOFA. Describe the offense.

TASHA. Should I start at the party?

VOFA. Describe the offense.

TASHA. Okay, um, well, we were at the end-of-year party in the gym and someone said we should play Spin-the-Bottle...

[*She continues to mouth words silently as* LIGHTS *go down on* TASHA'S *side and up on* ZED'S. *He is still crashing into walls and yelling.*]

ZED. TASHA! TASHA WHAT ARE THEY DOING TO YOU! YOU STUPID VOICE OF AUTHORITY YOU LET ME OUT! LET ME BE WITH TASHA!!

[LIGHTS *switch again*]

TASHA. I'd had a crush on Zed in the fifth grade, but not in sixth. In seventh he got taller and cuter and he was definitely back on my crush list. But he wasn't at the top, I mean, I didn't think I liked him that way—until the, you know, the thing you're calling "the offense."

VOFA. Tasha 3942, the Voice of Authority reminds you to stick to the topic.

TASHA. Well, pretty soon after we started playing Spin-the-Bottle, the guards came. It wasn't a big make-out session or anything, not in the gym in front of everyone! It was just a little kiss. I didn't even think about the fact that we were breaking the 2017 Bans. When we studied them at school we thought they were about marriage, not kissing! The guards put us on the detention bus and brought us here.

There was music on the bus, the same crappy music we get all day at school, but as we rode along, the music seemed... beautiful, more like real music you'd play on purpose in your room with your friends. And the view out the window was beautiful, too, like we could see each grain of sand outside and feel all the feelings of everything.

The best part was that Zed and I were having the same experience. I don't know how I know that but I do. Like, we were thinking together, seeing together. He moved his hand closer to mine at the exact moment I moved mine closer to his, and then we were holding hands, not looking at each other but totally blissed-out on the music and the view, the stupid boring music and the drab ugly view, I would have said the day before, but for us it was—I don't know how to explain it.

When the bus pulled up to the detention building the guards yelled at us to go into rooms eleven and twelve, but we both went into eleven. We were still holding hands, and then, we, like, fell into each other, and kissed some more. I don't know much about kissing, I mean really I don't know anything at all about kissing, but it was like we had to do it to feel normal. I know this is going to sound gross and weird but Zed's mouth tasted so good to me, it was like his saliva was the most delicious thing ever invented.

[*she pauses, as if hearing a sound*]

[LIGHTS *switch*]

ZED. TASHA!! YOU LET ME OUT YOU LET ME GET TO TASHA WHAT ARE YOU DOING TO HER [*etc., ad lib*]

[LIGHTS *switch*]

VOFA. Please continue.

TASHA. Did you hear something? I heard, like, pounding?

VOFA. Please continue describing the offense.

TASHA. Okay, okay. I'm pretty much done anyway. The guards came in and separated us, and put me in this room, where I am now with you and everyone watching me through this mirror [*gestures toward audience*], and I've been here for three days and I would like to know when you're going to let me go home. And I'd like to know when I can see Zed again. We are both well-adjusted students with good grades and neither of us has ever been in trouble before this.

VOFA. Do you promise to refrain from physical contact with Zed in the future?

TASHA. Um – I don't think I can promise that. Do I have to promise that to get out of here?

[VOFA *is silent.* LIGHTS *switch on in* ZED'S *room.* TASHA *and* ZED *go silent, looking out at the audience—they know that judgment time has come.*]

VOFA. Citizens, you have heard the testimony of Tasha 3942 and witnessed the behavior of Zed 5755. You must now decide if they will be permanently separated and punished, or if their offense will be forgiven.

As you know, when our Leader made America great again in 2017, he abolished the court system and so-called "civil rights." All legal decisions are now made by democratic vote, because democracy is terrific. The Voice of Authority reminds you that according to Executive Order 14983 the New American voting rules are as follows. Voting is a privilege and is not anonymous. You must be registered by race, religion, gender, and sexual orientation in order to vote. Heterosexual white Christian men have two votes each and may vote with two hands. All other men, reformed homosexuals, and white Christian women rated six and above have 5/8 of a vote and may raise their hands to the level of their heads. All other women have 3/8 of a vote and may raise their hands to the level of their chins. Pregnant women share their vote with the unborn child or children and therefore have zero votes. Gay, disabled, elderly, and first and second generation Americans have zero votes. Those who protested Executive Order 14983 have zero votes. If you lack a complete understanding of your voting status, you must not vote.

[LIGHTS *on in audience.*]

VOFA. We will now vote by show of hands. Shall we allow Tasha and Zed to continue at school together?

[*counts votes*]

Shall Tasha and Zed be separated and punished?

[*counts votes*]

[*If the audience votes to allow* TASHA *and* ZED *to remain together*]

VOFA. Tasha and Zed shall continue at school together.

[*Divider slides away and actors rush toward each other and embrace.*]

The Voice of Authority will keep a record of how each citizen voted. Some citizens may have their right to vote rescinded as a result of this process.

[If the audience votes to separate TASHA and ZED]

VOFA. Tasha and Zed shall be separated and punished.

[Divider remains in place with actors on either side, ZED sits down and begins to cry, and TASHA starts pounding on walls and shouting for ZED.]

The Voice of Authority thanks you for your participation in keeping America great.

Jessy Randall's work has appeared in Poetry, McSweeney's, and The Best American Experimental Writing. Her most recent book is *Suicide Hotline Hold Music* (Red Hen, 2016), a collection of poems and comics. The Offense is based on her short story *The Hedon-Ex Anomaly*, which first appeared in the science fiction magazine Lady Churchill's Rosebud Wristlet. Randall is a librarian at Colorado College and her website is http://bit.ly/JessyRandall.

The Suppressed

The end of the world again, well
here we are, monks beating on glass
with our bare skulls.

Observed behind glass this delicacy:
girls placing flowers on a grave.
The tears rolling down their cheeks

are little tanks. And all
we can accomplish
is prayer.

Oh history, inelegant stammerer,
do I hear that the nation of my hopes
goes under again?

John Morgan has published six books of poetry and a collections of essays. Winner of the Discovery Award of the New York Poetry Center, Morgan divides his time between Fairbanks, Alaska, and Bellingham, Washington. For more information visit his website: johnmorganpoet.com

From the protest

and maybe tonight our words will form a Golem and it will render our enemies small and we'll awaken God and He'll get back to all that smiting but with better aim this time and our boots will erode this whole city until everything on top bleeds into a desolate landslide that lasts only as long as this tide and the Kingdom of God will have meaning and Revelations will have meaning and it will be exactly the meaning we need it to have

or maybe our prayers are just bellowed hopes that never reach anyone capable of saving the harvest or waking the dead because maybe the Red Sea didn't part from the heavens but from the tremors of enough stamping feet and this is all we are, the loving embrace of an earthquake to its own shockwave, and we are the Golem, protecting ourselves from all of the eyes that only view us as mud.

Jew Boy White Boy

After Angel Nafis and Jon Sands

Jew boy white boy
For now
Jew boy born in 1981 Chicagoland
Jew boy born white boy

1971 Jew boys white boys
1961 Jew boys white boys
1951 Jew boys Jew boys
1941 Jew boys dead boys
1931 Jew boys white boys

2016 Jew boy write Jew boy
Oppression poem. Audience peeved
Because Jew boy
White boy

Jew boy white guilt
Jew boy Black Lives Matter rally
Jew boy pro-Palestine rally
But still take free trip to Israel
Jew boy pray at Wailing Wall
Not sure who he's praying to
Jew boy can't spell G-d
Jew boy atheist
And doesn't understand why that's so confusing
Jew boy care more about Drake being Jewish
Than God being Jewish

1471 Jew boy European boy
1481 Jew boy European boy
1491 Jew boy Jew boy
1492 Jew boy ash

Jew boy lights candles
But doesn't know the prayers
Jew boy atheist but still seek Jewish girl
Jew boy and Jew girl walk in 7 circles
Under godless chupah
Raise holy children
In godless house
Jew boy Jew girl
Have Jew boy

Jew boy white boy
Jew boy white boy
White boy Jew boy
White boy forget he Jew boy

For now

Eric Sirota hails from Champaign, Illinois, where he helps run a foreclosure defense Clinic and Elder Financial Justice Clinic at the University of Illinois College of Law. Eric also moonlights as a poet, three times earning a spot at the National Poetry Slam and twice earning a spot at the Individual World Poetry Slam. He wrote a poem about Cookie Monster that won an award from the Springfield Writers Guild. He also sometimes rants over beats and is part of the Rogue Tendency collective in Champaign, Illinois and The Nocturnals in Chicago, Illinois.

Music available at soundcloud.com/roguetendency.
You can't miss him. He's the tallest Jew for miles.

Holding My Husband

November 9, 2016

Holding my husband tight
this morning, giving
and receiving reassurance,
we do not speak. We know
who we are. We know what
we feel. In silence I wonder
is this how my parents felt
in 1933, when Hitler had
bullied his way into power
with a promise, among others,
to make Germany great again?
Did they hold each other
like this, full of terrible unease
trying for comfort? We are
only two small people doing
our best. We cannot stem this
tide. Everything will be all right.
It wasn't. Though much, much
later it was again. I love you,
world, even as you are
spinning out of control.

Beate Sigriddaughter, www.sigriddaughter.com, is poet laureate of Silver City, New Mexico (Land of Enchantment). Her work has received several Pushcart Prize nominations and poetry awards. In 2018 FutureCycle Press will publish her poetry collection *Xanthippe and Her Friends*.

Turn it Up

The thing about expectations is how quickly they can turn. We didn't see the full picture of who we were about to be until all those counties that were supposed to turn blue turned red. A fiery angry red, like whoever the colorist was at the TV station was mixing some black into the TV signal. That red, it couldn't have been angry enough.

I never thought it would happen. That we would go to an election party. That we would put the kids in the car, bring apple pies and bottles of champagne we never opened. That we would show up at a friends house to organize our lives around election night like it was some kind of entertainment.

It never felt like entertainment. It felt like we were hanging on to the last moments of the old world. That's what we were doing. We were so convinced of a Hillary win, we pre-bought the champagne. This was supposed to be Madame President's coronation, instead it was a trip to hell.

There was a moment my body started revolting. My stomach all tied up. Expectations, if we knew what was going to happen, we would've brought riot gear. We would've brought sleeping masks so our kids wouldn't have to see this. We weren't supposed to go through all of this in one night. That's how arrogant we were. My wife and I were prepared for victory. What it felt like to have half of a country turn on you like that, silent, invisible.

The next day at school was a hope hangover. I could hardly speak about photography without dropping a few tears. I wanted to speak and let my students know how much I supported them. My students, I love them all, but something had happened. Their voices said hello, but their bodies told me something else. They couldn't say it through their lips, but they said it with the turn of a shoulder. They were close, but we had become more distant. Stealth.

The people you thought could help you, who could never vote for a person like that. It was already happening on the street before it happened in your nightmares.

And when the news came over the wire, when the papa who calls this whole election, called his boss, said this is who we want. Go ahead and let everyone know. We made this. We took our outrage and blew up his distorted message until his distorted message became the message played on every radio and newspaper cover. Go to the grocery store, there it will be. Log onto social media, you'll see it there too.

Don't tell me about checks and balances and decency and how the solution for all of this is that we should all just get along, to move past your own anger. You didn't try to step in and change things. The system was broken so you made it more broken. It wasn't enough to just complain, you had to not vote too.

Did you think that Hillary would just win, that you didn't have to think about it? You just treated election day like every other encounter of racism that you encounter, that you don't say anything about, you moved on with your life, because at the end of the day it's all about you.

I first heard the term Police Brutality from Hip Hop. NWA's Straight Outta Compton to be specific in Miami, 1991. High school, my hip hop education. I lived in a rich neighborhood. I went to private school. I was one of them except I wasn't.

Ice T and the movie "Colors." Chuck D and what he taught me about institutional racism. How the giants of my parents lives, weren't saints, *Elvis was a racist simple and plain.* I didn't see it walking around. I was so privileged, seeing a world only a few had access to. In the 1980s I didn't have a political consciousness, I had Michael Stipe, I had Bono, I had Chuck D, Ice Cube, and Ice-T. I learned mine from them. Their outrage became my outrage. And now, where is Chuck D now to process this new regime for me? I wanted all of the teachers who ever taught me anything about myself to be there for me, to help me process what has happened, a shoulder for me to cry on.

But the truth is none of my teachers can save me. There is no music to explain what happened, how we as a society could so quickly fall apart, and it was never so quick. Things are invisible until they aren't. The older we get, the more our idols die, the more we need to fill our lives with our own protests.

The time has come to make our own meanings out of what we've been taught. We live in a world where the most listened to people in our society are not the wisest, but the loudest, that's who wins out. The political climate of the 1980s is coming back, only now it's much much worse. But we have amazing tools we never had in the 1980s. And after everything, we still have words and sounds, our words, our sounds, our anger. Our words and sounds they can be a fist, they can be a middle finger. They made this and we have to fix it. We have our hearts, we have our children, who we've raised on decency and kindness. It's up to us as parents, and teachers, to be the person music was for me in the 1980s. I have to be the Chuck D for my daughters, for my students, for anyone who'll listen. The time is now. This music will be loud. *Turn it up.*

Adam Strong is a high school digital arts teacher. Adam Strong is the founder of the reading series, Songbook PDX. His work has appeared in Nailed Magazine, Intellectual Refuge and in the anthology City of Weird. He writes and loves in Portland, OR.

WHEN POLITICS ARE THICKER THAN BLOOD

It is so easy

To explain how this happens.
In stories and books
Empires rise and fall in a few sentences.
But it is so hard to look your kid in the face.

What You Are at War With

-Normalization
-What you feel vs what is true
-Role models and positions of power as dangerously low ceilings
-The white student I had who wrote the N word on the bottom of his journal entry
-How it was a small town, and when I told the assistant director of the learning center where I taught the class, he explained to me about how it was a small town, and how that student probably had never met any black people ever, and how he was just a dumb kid trying to impress his friends, and to take it easy on him
-How I hope he reads this and knows what a piece of shit he is, and that I will never be off the hook for how I let him off the hook
-I scolded him and sent him a picture of my cousin's family, who is black, and I said that the lives of these beautiful kids will be harder because of people like you
-Life is an equation now and we have to determine where we were that factored into it
-It's 2017 now. We have more than 4 years
-We have forever
-I want you to know that, I said, like it was on a grave
-Not life and death, but what life is:
-Your friends
-Your families
-Yourself
-People pass through graveyards like symbols, like how you might do flashcards
-Because death is guaranteed, but what is life?
-What is life, really?
-What really is life?

Russell Jaffe is the editor of TL;DR magazine (tldrmagazine.com). He is the author of four poetry collections, most recently *La Croix Water* (Damask, '16) and *Civil Coping Mechanisms* (Civil Coping Mechanisms, forthcoming '17). He is a real dad doing real things. The work included here is from a greater collection called *In the American Rubble*.

Wishes for Emily in the Age of Trump

Let her be the daydreamer
at the tidal pool, her fingers stroking
the splayed wings of pectoral fins,
her ears tuning in to the argot of the tongue-tied
and tongue-less, the clicking of crustaceans
and the grunts and groans of swim bladders.
Let her be as open as a starfish unfurling
to a birdless sky, an ebbing tide.
Let her make a vow to a beloved
on a switchback trail and fall asleep
with pine sap in her hair.

And let her be a collector of feathers,
a follower of snail trails, a sideways girl
listening for footfalls in the maze.
Let her be the bow, not the arrow.
The linden, not the felling ax.

Let her pick her own words,
          slick and lustrous,
                    from the stream beds and salt marshes,
and from the mice prints in the snow:
hop   tail drag   hop   hush   and scatter.

When scolded for her sensitivity,
let her make art. Let her record her fevers,
her frisson in the old-growth forest,
her contempt for the badmouths
and demagogues with their drone bombs
and misdirection.

          And let her find her own way
out of that moneyed talent contest called America
with its black magician stage and embarrassment
of corporate lights tangling
its edges like chains.

Sarah Giragosian's poems have recently appeared in Ecotone, Best of the Net Anthology, Prairie Schooner, The Missouri Review, The Baltimore Review, Blackbird, and Verse Daily, among others. A winner of the 2014 American Poetry Journal Book Prize, her first book, *Queer Fish,* is available from Dream Horse Press. She teaches in the department of Writing and Critical Inquiry at the University at Albany-SUNY.

Seed

My son's favorite time of year is autumn.
We walk around the neighborhood in the evenings
And he points out every pumpkin he sees.
"Pun-kin!" "Pun-kin!"
We find them at doors and on porches.
On windows and cars.
On TV screens.
"Pun-kin!"
No, honey
That's not a pumpkin.
That's the man who wants to lead our country.
A man who wants to be looked up to
As the example we see framed
Over classroom doors.
The same man who told us all
He could grab women by the pussy.
That his mouth
Was a magnet
To their bodies.
That he couldn't control himself.

My son thinks this man is a pumpkin.
He doesn't see that behind the jack-o-lantern grin
There is something rotting.
That the words this man speaks
Could be his dictionary.

I think of the man who grabbed me
Pulled me into an alley
And touched my skin.
Who called me "devil"
Because I tempted his hands
Who told his friends
That my still, unmoving body
Was the worst sex he ever had.

I think
Will my son
Fill his own head
With seeds too big to swallow

And then choke those around him
Because one man
This man
Told him
They all loved the feeling
Of being silenced?

Melissa Rose has been writing and performing poetry since 2001. She began hosting community spoken word and slam poetry events in 2003 and since then has been a member of 5 national poetry slam teams. She is currently the Executive Director of Siren, an organization that empowers girls and women through spoken word.

Angry Bird - March 18
Geoffry Smalley

Robert Pfeiffer

To My Daughter, After Trump

Sweet Girl, I'm afraid
everything I want you to believe
about the world is a lie.
Last night, your country decided
this man, who does not believe
you even deserve his respect,
this man, who does not believe
you even deserve equality,
should be *your* president.

This morning I left in a haze,
before dawn. You were sleeping
beside your mother, congestion
clicking softly in your chest.
Warm, safe, your world
will still seem the same –
breakfast, preschool, swimming. But.

Everything you already are,
and everything we hope
you to be—curious, loving,
kind in a way that can rupture
the cold shell of cynicism—
we still want for you. But.
I cannot point to *that* man
as an example of anything
we hope for you to find in this life.

Even if the pyre of human decency
seems to await his next match,
know this: We *must* love
or nothing else matters.
Be good, even if the world is not.
Be kind, even if the world is not.
Be soft in the hard world
even if, especially if, it hurts.
Love boldly. Cynicism is easy.
Hatred is cowardly. Be brave.

Sweet Girl, you are too good for this.
It's dark this morning. But,
I'm heading out into it, for you.

Robert Pfeiffer received his MFA and PhD in Creative Writing from Georgia State University. His first collection of poems, *Bend, Break*, was published in 2011 by Plain View Press, and his second, *The Inexhaustible Before* is forthcoming. Individual poems have appeared in Mudfish, Iodine Poetry Journal, The Haight Ashbury Literary Journal, The Flint Hills Review, and The Fourth River among others. He is an Associate Professor of English at Clayton State University, and lives in Decatur, Georgia with his wife, daughter, and two dogs.

The Hinge

Forgive
the craft
of pouring myself
into pitchers.

Water
cannot tolerate thirst
for long periods
of time, the thirst

that invaded my homeland
during the years
of submarginal
words.

Politicians
burned down
the charity bazaars
and school libraries.

Now my son
will inherit
a handful of ashes.

Sergio A. Ortiz is a gay Puerto Rican poet and the founding editor of Undertow Tanka Review. He is a two-time Pushcart nominee, a four-time Best of the Web nominee, and 2016 Best of the Net nominee. He won 2nd place in the 2016 Ramón Ataz annual poetry competition, sponsored by Alaire Publishing House. He is currently working on his first full-length collection of poems, *Elephant Graveyard*.

When politics are thicker than blood

I went to my father with my heart in my hands. Told him how terrified I was. Reminded him of the beautiful black and brown people in our family. Of all the kinds of diversity we contain. Asked him to step up and stand beside me against hate.

He failed.

His failure was one of complacency, of an aversion to conflict, of the illusion of safety that comes with following a lead that seems stronger than your own. I am certain there was no intention of harm in his choice, but he aligned himself with hate, like so many people who confuse status quo with eminent domain. Like the ones that founded this country, and thought trees and water and land and bodies were theirs to use and sell and discard.

That vote helped to give the reins of power to a man currently pending trial for the rape of an underage girl, and a man that wants to electroshock me into compliance and control my body. Those men are being emulated all across the country this week as women's bodies are assaulted and queer and trans bodies are assaulted and people of color become, horrifically, even more of a target.

I spend my days working at a Trans and Queer clinic, and I can tell you without a single doubt that since those polls spiked into red, people have been terrified. Are considering suicide, or fleeing the country. Are sure that they will lose their medication, their reproductive choices, and the chance to live as themselves. We are racing to find answers to anguished questions while wiping tears from our own frightened faces.

My father chose the party line over my well being. I cannot escape that knowledge. It crawls up the back of my neck to nest at the base of my skull, next to the fear of being raped and the knowledge that my body is not as strong or as fast as it used to be. It keeps pulling my hands into fists and my stomach into knots until I'm shaking and pacing and trying to remember how to breathe. Looking up self defense classes. Keeping my back to the wall.

This is only the second day.

I keep reminding myself that this is not new; that this kind of virulent hatred has spread for centuries and terrorizes people with less privilege than me every day. That I was never really safe, just less obviously at risk. That at least white people know now the true extent of our collective dysfunction, and how motivating it could be to come together to finally undo the damage and unlearn the bigotry. I am committed to this fight.

I am also fighting to stay present in my body like I haven't for decades. I have also fully assessed my willingness to go down fighting, and not just for sake of my own skin. I'm afraid for my friends and family who are people of color, who are Jewish, who are queer and trans and disabled. I'm afraid for my people in Arizona, but I don't fool myself that Oregon is any less dangerous. The sirens have been screaming all day and my news feed is full of stories of brazen daylight assaults.

With the usual American arrogance, we have done this to ourselves. Land of the free, we say, and then turn people into prison labor, deport families, and bomb the country they barely escaped from. Home of the brave, we say, using our national guard to protect corporate interests and attack American citizens, ignoring the veterans on the streets, the children dying of hunger and disease and abuse, holy when a fetus but not after.

We are liars.

We lie to ourselves all the time. We buy and sell the lies. We agree to them, wear them, torture our bodies for them, fight for them, pray to them. Even elect them.

So here we are. No more comforting facade of safety or fairness. Public permission given to hate with both hands. Dividing lines like fractures, with some family on the other side. Rage and fear like molten rock between, but they try to say the burn is incidental. That they aren't splashing the magma, they just agree with some of its melting points. That the ash we're choking on isn't personal.

My father chose something else over my safety. Knowing full well the dangers of men drunk on violence and unchecked by rules, he cast that vote. Knowing almost nothing about what I've already survived because he never asked, he cast that vote. Knowing the views of his church and how deadly they can be with law behind them, he cast that vote.

I came to my father with my heart in my hands, and he didn't pause to consider it. Didn't note how fragile the ribs that guard it, or the seams running every which way. Didn't ask about numb spots, or the stutters in the beat. Didn't offer his hand to curl around it, helping me keep it safe. Just gave me some platitudes, a side step or two, and an empty space where the hate could creep through.

I will grieve for my lost father while I try to survive this patriarchy. Is that irony, or just a damn shame?

He will likely never know the ferocious beauty that is my community striving to hold each other up; to build treasure out of scraps and determination; to keep each other alive. He will likely never know the best parts of me, or understand my sacred, or see me clearly. He is on the far side of that fractured foundation, and we may never meet again.

Sossity Chiricuzio is a queer femme outlaw poet, and a working class storyteller, what her friends' parents often referred to as a bad influence, and possibly still do. A 2015 Lambda Fellow, she writes as activism, connection, and survival. She is a contributing columnist at PQmonthly. com, and half of the performance duo Sparkle & Truth. Her work has appeared in a variety of publications including Adrienne, great weather for MEDIA, Lunch Ticket, and NANO fiction, as well as anthologies like The Remedy: Queer And Trans Voices On Health And Health Care, Glitter and Grit: Queer Performance from the Heels on Wheels Femme Galaxy, and Procyon Science Fiction Anthology 2016. Find more at sossitywrites.com.

...Only the Past, Happening Over and Over Again

I come from a very large, Greek-American family. Most of us are inclusive in life and in our politics. As a whole, we're a loving, courageous, welcoming group. My generation won the Chronological Lottery and grew up affluent in the U.S. Many of our forebears lived under Nazi occupation in Greece and then through the subsequent Greek civil war. My paternal grandfather was in the Greek resistance and fought Nazis, and my paternal grandmother died at 26 under Nazi occupation when my dad was six. We don't know where her remains lie; just that they were tossed into an unmarked mass grave. We don't even know her birthday because the Nazis burned the town's records.

Yet somehow, I have at least five family members who voted for DJT. They know history, they have graduate degrees, they have means. They know I've been disabled by Myalgic Encephalomyelitis for 25 years and that one of our cousins is wheelchair-bound because of Multiple Sclerosis. Through us, they've witnessed how even highly accomplished disabled persons are treated differently. I believe they would take a bullet for either of us; they couldn't, however, change their political allegiance.

I started writing and calling my Congressional representatives when I was 14 and have done so my entire life. I've marched for Black Lives Matter and Seattle Stands with Standing Rock on my crutches. I was a Domestic Violence Victim Advocate in my twenties and began volunteering for the LGBTQ community in 1994. I know how to fight smart and fight hard. Now I actively resist DJT and his supporters in Congress, for obvious moral and sociopolitical reasons, and because I love my young nephew so much. Literally and metaphorically, he deserves the safest possible climate. I will ALWAYS love those in my family who voted for DJT. Always. But I don't see them the same way. They know this. And they no longer see me the same way. They think I'm "making too big of a deal of it" and that I'm "not giving him a chance." I'm undeterred, but my heart is broken in places I thought would always remain intact.

I continue to study and learn from those who fought harder battles and won. I cry (sob, some days) then keep at it. But I know my relationship with some of my family is irrevocably altered. I never thought an election could do that to us.

Litsa Dremousis is the author of *Altitude Sickness* (Future Tense Books). Seattle Metropolitan Magazine named it one of the all-time "20 Books Every Seattleite Must Read." She is an essayist with The Washington Post and her work appears in myriad publications.

David Romtvedt

Election Night in Wyoming

The sky thickening, not so much
like chocolate in a double boiler
as mud sliding down a hillside
and burying a house at the bottom—
the smell, pulpy wood and falling hair,
cancer, untouchable, the harbor
called hope. The odds are bad, high,
and we all die in the end. Even me
drinking chocolate, waiting out
another election night, the wind
blowing and the snow falling
from unseen heights. My mother
and father, long dead, sit beside me,
counseling—not too worry, all things
are blown away in the end, but I can't
feel the way they do. I'm alive
and the votes are being counted.
The mud slowly hardens as the
temperature drops. Do I have
cancer? I might have cancer.
Cancer is everywhere, sweeping
across the dark sky.

Hearing the President Speak

New snow falling on old,
masking the smell of the earth.

Sunlight silver across the corniced ridgeline,
rising toward becoming, nearly cloud.

A chickadee in the spruce, calling,
moose at the window, waiting.

Wood cutting, the blade churning,
sawdust settling on snow, smoldering.

Wind from the north, making the flags
leap from the poles, the edges tearing.

Winter—it's hard to remember
summer, or spring, burning the ditches.

Even here in Wyoming, far
from policy, there is fear.

David Romtvedt is a poet and musician. With the band, Ospa he recently finished a recording of traditional Basque music of Wyoming and the Basque Country. His most recent books are a collection of poems, *Dilemmas of the Angels* (Louisiana State University Press, 2017), and the novel *Zelestina Urza in Outer Space* (University of Nevada Center for Basque Studies, 2015).

Marty McConnell

the patriot

In a dice game, there is no pie.
No pie in a clabber clobber bottle,
in a drought, empty thirst, no pie.
No pie in a cactus, or a pear, or
a smooth coat of otters, in austerity,
in France, no pie. No pie
in Jesus, no pie in kings, no pie
in barters or conquerings or nests
of wasps slumbering through February
no pie in teapots or their cozies no pie in TV
shows where the protagonist is a serial
killer but made some ways sympathetic, no pie
in cement mixers, no pie in nurseries
full of shrubbery and perennials and assorted
flowering genuses of greenery that produce
no fruit no human-size shadow no waiting tins
of sweet hot salted American coagulation.

the sin of anticipatory distress

Heavy wine in my hand and already I'm wondering
what's next. What resembling forgetting can I put
in my body to lose this year or its edges. Who'd wish
to lose a year? Cars slush past. The sky's a dark fence
between us and the heaven we invent to yes our existence.
It's not even as brutal yet as it's going to get.

the sacrament of hope after despair

How many men must we survive? The fortysomething
at the screen door when I was 15. Roses on the porch
whenever Dad was out of town. The one who tried to
rape me. The other one who tried to rape me. The one
who lied and dissolved and lied and dissolved and lied
until I left, then followed me home to lie again. The
one who made me and broke my mother's heart. The
ones with the perfect syllables concealing machetes.
Getting hard pursuing ruin. The ones with the gun
racks and sweet guitars. The ones rolling promotions
in their suit pant pockets like loose change. The ones
who lisp Audre Lorde quotes over top shelf bourbon
as if the beds they rose from to come here aren't full
of women who used to have hands. Not all men, but
enough. Enough.

> Oh my nephews. Oh my godson.
> You do not have to be women to be
> kind. Look at your fathers, wounded
> by their own fathering, how they
> make tea and hold you. Destroying
> nothing. Killing no one.

Marty McConnell is the author of *wine for a shotgun*; *when they say you can't go home again, what they mean is you were never there*, (winner of the 2017 Michael Waters Poetry Prize and forthcoming in 2018); and *Gathering Voices: Creating a Community-Based Poetry Workshop*, forthcoming in 2018 on YesYes Books.

Laura Foley

Corked

We queue in bright November sun,
outside Town Hall,
beaming our innocence.
That night, we take
a savored bottle from the fridge,
chill two fluted glasses,
keep the bottle closed
and wait.
At eight, my daughter texts:
I'm worried, and I respond:
It's early, Dear,
the states will soon turn blue.
At ten, she texts again:
When will it be
not early?
I wonder too,
all Election Day, and the next,
while the champagne
stays under pressure.

On Refusing Anesthetic

For three hours,
the scalpel does its cutting:
I lie unflinching,
practice meditation,
follow my breath,
slow in, slow out.
The hardest part,
I tell the doctor,
is the waiting room,
incessant TV barking
I'm not used to,
tidbits of the latest murder
blaring from the screen,
a thoughtless Tweet
repeated from our president-elect—
senseless acts for which
I would accept
any numbing possible.

Laura Foley is the author of five poetry collections. *The Glass Tree* won the Foreword Book of the Year Award, Silver, and was a Finalist for the New Hampshire Writer's Project, Outstanding Book of Poetry. *Joy Street* won the Bi-Writer's Award. Her poems have appeared in journals and magazines including Valparaiso Poetry Review, Inquiring Mind, Pulse Magazine, Poetry Nook, Lavender Review, The Mom Egg Review and in the British Aesthetica Magazine. She won Harpur Palate's Milton Kessler Memorial Poetry Award and the Grand Prize for the Atlanta Review's International Poetry Contest.

No Vacancy

While Driving to San Luis Obispo, My Mother Tells Me She Stopped Listening to Music after George W. Bush Stole the Presidency

'Cause it seemed to her that all the radio was good for
was listening to democracy take itself apart
speech by speech
soldier by soldier
    day by day
until all that was left was static in the air
until all that was left was two babies and a husband
until all that was left was a day to get through
My mom tells me she stopped listening to anything that didn't have
  "public" somewhere in its name 'cause she was tired of secrets
    And God knows NPR ain't got nothing on the West
it just squats on the beach rolling in its almost-heaven
we hug the coastline like we're supposed to
When I was in grade school I remember crying
after my first iPod got stolen 'cause now I'd have to walk to class in silence
and to my left there is a man on a kayak
floating just outside of the shore's reach
I wonder if he can swim
I wonder if he's made peace with his dependence
on this thing we call the ocean
My grandma sings hymns when she cleans the house
My Mom has the TV on when she cleans the house: In this way
I have learned to swim
I have made peace with my dependence on this thing we call music
My mother asks me who I'm voting for
I lie and tell her I haven't thought about it
I ask her what song she'd want to hear right now if she had her choice
  she lies and tells me she hasn't thought about it
The kayak is gone
and I promise to make her a mix CD before the election

Track 5: Green Day – American Idiot

Everyone wants to know the fate of the earth, but no one wants to learn it alone, so me & Megan gather a group of people & walk across campus to the only mecca this place can afford under the cover of a night so black it ain't seen kids as old as us in years

& none of us are really friends; Me & Megan are the only two hinges between all of us & no one really knows each other & ain't that what I'm always saying? That people are just Venn diagrams covered in skin & filled with blood born from legacy or a legacy born from blood & ain't I the one that's always saying that you can only ever come from one place? But no one wants to hear me talk about that shit right now 'cause we just want to know who our next president is going to be

So we do as we have been taught: we colonize the back of the room & order pizza & make jokes about walls & toupees & the color orange & across the room I can see a tide of red oozing across the country, pinned up & glowing on the TV; Kentucky, Arizona, Arkansas & every few minutes I walk across the room to the people brave enough to keep score & I ask *How's it going?* & they say *I think you know* & then I ask *How are you doing?* & they say *I think you know*

& we are still essentially kids; we still live among the rubble of a whole that ain't been whole since our parents graduated & there was nothing left to do but break pieces into pieces so there would always be something left to get done 'cause we woke up in this world craving a good meal & lacking any kind of compass & maybe our parents just didn't want to die alone & maybe our parents got tired of running & so they sculpted new legs out of whatever heat they could build between them & maybe being young ain't as good as being able to look back on being young but regardless we still gotta break something: silence, bones, the rules

I vote for tension so every time I return to our table I stop & look Megan dead in the eye & sing *I'm not part of the redneck agenda* really badly as if that line would offer enough hope to spread over everyone here tonight & she laughs every time & by badly I mean my voice cracks over every word & the cracks look like state lines & the red ain't heard a voice soaked in so much desperate glee since my great great great great grandfather tried to stay alive by throwing his own songs out across the vast slaughterhouse of the red's backyard like a sprinkler in Alabama, Texas, Indiana

The red don't stop for us the red don't care about us the red knocks on every door in Ohio & just enough people let it in to start believing it lived there this whole time & when I see this on the TV I miss my pizza by a mile & a half & bite into the meat of my lip & maybe you too are tired of everyone comparing injustice to a storm or a fire or a flood but I bite my lip & the blood starts swimming the blood never stops the blood is a sprinkler the blood is somebody's daddy singing loud enough for everyone to hear the blood just wants to be seen so it turns the whole state red

& then a campus security guard turns off the TV & becomes surrounded by a field of violent booing & I say *we wanted to see what was going to happen* & he says *I think you know* so Megan and I turn & leave & the funny part is that he was old & black the funny part is he's seen all this before; the kids & the race & the hopeful laughter & I'm not saying all black people weren't shocked by the red's conquest but I am saying that Megan had to look up what par for the course meant when I explained why I only cry after I've comforted everyone else & come Wednesday campus was grey & empty, everybody a ghost, or else pretending to be.

Gyasi Hall is a poet from Columbus, Ohio. He is currently the poetry editor of Otterbein University's Literary Magazine, Quiz and Quill, and has seen his work published and produced in various places, including Z Publishing's Best Emerging Poets of Ohio Anthology, and Get Lit's first poetry textbook. He wants to talk to you about your favorite albums.

The Day America Turned Red

Election day was blue. The sky.

I flew from Chicago to New York. The landing: also blue. I had a job interview, I voted at dusk at PS 165 on 109th in New York, admiring its chalky blue stripe. I remembered the lady poll worker from the primaries, she smiled and said she was glad we are neighbors. I told her we aren't anymore: I am just registered to vote with the address once shared with a gone thing. We shared a blue moment.

I bought milk on the way home from the bodega where the owner calls me *princess habibi*. I Googled this just to see the results: "PRINCESS BLUE hookah" on Amazon. When I came home there was red. The polls. My period started. I put in a menstrual cup and also a pad on although I never need both, and I took two klonopin and an ambien with some wine because I do not own the princess blue hookah. The siren outside was red, the light was blue. My room is cream so it became both. I spiraled patriotic into quiet:

> What is it like to be a woman listening in the dark? Black mantle of silence stretches between them like geothermal pressure. Ascent of the rapist up the stairs seems as slow as lava. She listens to the blank space where his consciousness is, moving towards her. Lava can move as slow as nine hours per inch. Color and fluidity vary with its temperature from dark red and hard (below 1,800 degrees centigrade) to brilliant yellow and completely fluid (above 1,950 degrees centigrade). She wonders if he is listening too. The cruel thing is, she falls asleep listening.
> — *The Autobiography of Red*, Anne Carson

I wake up to red. My period streaked across the sheets like watercolor from my legs running in a fitful red dream. I have never had such a heavy one. The map is all red. I cry and that is not red, but I am heat-ridden with a scarlet fury, a deep navy blanket of whatever is shock-mute, like night hanging over a trench. I am cream so I become both.

Outside it is gray. Two different people text me "even the sky is mourning." Is grief gray? *No,* I think, *likely brown.* I think of black living. I think of brown people streaked across the streets like watercolor, running in a fitful red nightmare; I think of the blood inside them. Their fast hearts now. I think of a white man's PR team deciding on a tie, *hmm, blue or red?* I think of the blue hours I have held a girl and watched the dawn, thinking *twilight lovers* are for blue hearts, and because of the blue on my map, I could paint the town red with my!! very!! crimson!! love!! My very fast girl heart, my very red girl part, my very blue blue art.

Did you know it is the 78th anniversary of Kristallnacht? It was blue that night but no one would know because the glass reflected all the light and the flames were red so it became the color of a scream. I think of my organic aborting, of that seed in me that could grow a little red tendril of thingness, of the red anger from red cities who would rather me blue and bloated, my cream Potential milking up the waiting room coffee, the ink in an insurance-doesn't-cover-it pen white enough that the words don't appear on paper.

"Something there is that doesn't love a wall," wrote Frost, and it mattered because the ink was dark. "I will go quiet into that good night," says a man behind the wall, and it does not matter because he is brown.

The colors do not know for whom they stand. You cannot blame them [the colors] for being. I ask the white, *why?* but it does not speak, it answers in blue or red or glass that reflects both:

in the last red light of the year
that knows what it is, that knows it's neither
ice nor mud nor winter light
but wood, with a gift for burning
   —*Song*, Adrienne Rich

Perhaps what we must do with the vast is boil it down to the components of its own flag, to the minutiae of our daily ways of folding it into ourselves. If you paint Mona Lisa by her numbers she does not look so awfully complex. If you look at the colors in one Black Wednesday, what greater proof is there of Pangea? Kill the sense-making because it was already killed. Deport your fear. Build a wall around your unwillingness to listen. Trust the red swell within you, not the parted sea, the whole one. Trust the bluebird warbling in the ear of every person you pass on your watercolor street, because did you know this is the 78th anniversary of the structural failure of empathy?

157. The part I do remember: that the blue of the sky depends on the darkness of empty space behind it. As one optics journal puts it, "The color of any planetary atmosphere viewed against the black of space and illuminated by a sunlike star will also be blue." In which case blue is something of an ecstatic accident produced by void and fire."
   —*Bluets,* Maggie Nelson

On this red year that is wood with a gift for burning, I fist my hands up into blue, as an ecstatic accident, produced by void and fire. I trust women of color. I paint the flag by its numbers. I ask the other white, *why?* and to tell us the truth about the rainbow and how once a rabbi dyed the hands of each person in the shtetl a different color to catch the thief,

Everyone was quick to accuse Irwin P of running his brown hands up and down the Dial. He's so selfish! They said. He wants everything for himself! But it was their hands, all of their hands, a compressed rainbow of every citizen in the shtetl who had prayed for handsome sons, a few more years of life, protection from lightning, love... it was impossible to tell what had been touched by human hands and what was as it was because it was at was... when the blush of the schoolgirl's cheeks was mistaken for the crimson of the holy man's fingers, it was the schoolgirl who was called hussy, tramp, slut.
    —*Everything is Illuminated,* Jonathan Safran Foer

It was all of us.

Koby Liliana Omansky is a recent graduate of Sarah Lawrence College, where she was an undergraduate reader at the Sarah Lawrence College Poetry Festival, and was the recipient of the Harle Adair Damann Writing Award, and the Andrea K. Willison Poetry Prize for poetry that explores the relationships among women and justice. Her work has been published in Skin Deep Magazine, cliffhanger, The Decolonizer, and The Establishment. She lives and works in New York City with her close Chihuahua-ian collaborator, Goose.

Stopped At Customs, JFK, 2017

Maybe because the pattern on my shirt
is not the stars and stripes I've been
pergatoried upon Arrival. Others run
past my terminal but I am to be interrogated

by Immigration on how American am I.
My social media searched through, I can recite
each state capital, name three American desserts—
apple, pecan, Boston cream. Whoopee!

The interrogator reads my passport for place
of birth, he'll say a country I've had to detach from,
that is only part of my identity and what is the rest?
The interrogator says I am Muslim. I have been

living the American dream—working at a nail salon,
the life Horatio Alger wrote about. America
is where I'm being terrorized. Home is
where I was civil-warred. Immigration

tells me I'm a security concern, tells
me America isn't worldly anymore,
isn't promising, America has turned
its back on that.

Alexis Ivy's most recent poems have appeared in Spare Change News, Borderlands: Texas Poetry Review, J Journal and The Worcester Review. Her first poetry collection, *Romance with Small-Time Crooks,* was published in 2013 by BlazeVOX [books]. She is a Street Outreach Advocate in her hometown Boston.

Villanelle for Airport Travel, Winter 2017

Under snow, the barricade,
Fluorescent violet–white and gray;
My love, my heart, I am afraid.

The Fountain Bar in flowing span,
L'Occitane, Sanrio, Spanx, Chick-fil-A;
Under snow, the barricade.

The spacecraft gleam, the bullet tram,
Those lurching home who can or may;
My love, my heart, I am afraid.

Swift blue shapes remove a man
Who stumbles, cuffed, against the way;
Under snow, the barricade.

P.F. Chang, Be Relax, Hudson News, Auntie Anne,
Duty Free, Tech for Takeoff, Aveda, EA;
My love, my heart, I am afraid.

Four years of this or more at hand,
Of tracking blood to work and play—
Under snow, the barricade:
My love, my heart, I am afraid.

L.T. Patridge, originally from Greenville, Mississippi, recently received her MFA from the Writing & Publishing program at Vermont College of Fine Arts in Montpelier. She writes historical fiction and dark fantasy, including the upcoming novel *The Innsmouth Ladies' Book of Household Management*. She lives in Massachusetts.

Once, When They Knocked
with a nod to Italo Calvino

There was once a place
on the map called America,
shaped a lot like a hand
poised to knock on the door.

America was filled with
little towns not much more
than somewhere to post
a letter, buy a few gallons of gas
as you were passing through.

America housed larger towns too,
entire cities of cars ratcheting
along impacted roads,
streets with buildings so tall
they scratched the stars.

That was before number 45 took
office, before staged terror,
and nuclear assaults
of the constitution,
before neighbors took up
arms against neighbors.

That was when prayer
was legal no matter
who your gods,
or how you dressed
to address them,
and all expressions
of love, holy.

When a woman's body
was not cattle.

There was a place
called America, once,

where when we knocked
on the door, they said hello,
hello, come on in,
we've got soup on the stove,
enough for everyone.

Lana Hechtman Ayers resides in Oregon, where she enjoys clean rain, copious wildlife, and unpolluted sky thanks to the tireless folks at all the environmental agencies working for a better planet and better future for all beings. She holds an MFA in Poetry and in Fiction, and a Master's in Counseling Therapy.

Ester Prudlo

No Vacancy

There is no Statue of Liberty at the Rio Grande,
No light of welcome.

Maybe, at night—a torch or two like burning crosses,
before Civil Rights Sites were considered assets
to attract tourists to Montgomery, Alabama.

Desert trails do not lead to Plymouth Rock.
No friendly Native Americans
teach tired strangers how to plant corn.

Hundred and sixty acre plots are not
offered to anyone willing to build
a sod house and work the land.
These tired and thirsty strangers are
hand-cuffed and turned around
right now—or later.

We no longer lift a lamp to people
yearning to breathe free—

Our sign has been flipped over.
It says, "Go Away."

Ester Hauser Laurence Prudlo is the author of children's books, fiction, and non-fiction articles. Her poems have appeared in VerseWisconsin, Madison Magazine, Birmingham Arts Journal, Postcards & Prose, Lummox. New Mirage Journal. She taught creative writing courses with U of Wis. Ex. A retired counselor to soldiers and inmates, she and husband, Tony, now spend summers in Wisconsin and winters in Alabama.

Tod Marshall

America

was beautiful: a meadow for the horse with muscular white flanks,
galloping through grass, standing in sunlight, glossy mane shimmering
and glowing ivory against the blue sky, perhaps a cardinal landing
on a blossoming tree branch
                                    gluttony first, resentments, spending
hours seething at perceived misdeeds, became the tribe in red hats
spending day after long day straightening bent nails we'd pulled
out of old boards to reuse in the next supposedly impenetrable fence.

Tod Marshall has three books of poetry, most recently *Bugle* (Canarium 2014). He teaches at Gonzaga University, and from 2016–18 he served as the Washington State Poet Laureate.

While Walking in the Butterfly Pavilion
for Luke

Mexican blue wing butterflies
like shade over light, have bodies
that are dark not bright, hover
over bark not blooms, find ways

of scaling any wall, no matter
how tall, just like migrants
we call, *illegal* will. When a
government builds 600 miles

of fencing in the lower Rio Grande
River Valley, substituting
a hard border for the forest
butterflies are used to they

lose a kind of law & order,
nesting & flight patterns
disturbed. For some it means
a slight detour in the middle

of a 2,000 mile pilgrimage,
for many others it means
nothing less than the loss
of a village, homing instincts

rendered useless as a broken
GPS. No one really means
to pillage, of course, simply
hoping to keep those other

immigrants from going north.
Their names come from
humans: *Checkered White,*
Northern Cloudywing, Texas

Powdered Skipper, Dark Kite
Swallowtail, Mimosa Yellow,
& border bandits, field rats,
tire huggers, wetbacks: One

way or another these parts of
ourselves we give names to
always get in, migrate north
of any place we've ever been

to, reclaim those
forgotten names
we left behind:
butterfly, mariposa.

Rick Benjamin believes in ancient wisdom, like, say, a verse from the Tao de Ching that begins, "If you want to be a leader, let go of control." He also believes in circulating wisdom, daily and always through poetry. He is the former state poet laureate of Rhode Island (2012 – 2016), and has published three books of poetry—*Passing Love* (2010), *Floating World* (2013), and *Endless Distances* (2015). He believes deeply in resistance and resilience.

They Are Running Toward My Mother

My cousin Lela in Toronto tells me immigrants
are arriving in Canada minus fingers and toes.
Some are crossing frozen fields at relaxed
stretches along the border between North Dakota
and Manitoba, fleeing America like Eliza did
in *Uncle Tom's Cabin* from a related disease,
treading ice with her baby in her arms wrapped
in a shawl. Lela really called to see how Laura's
doing after back surgery, but we slip into Trump
talk inevitably. That was several days ago, though
these days are one long night. Tonight, after walking
under clouds spitting rain, small drops landing
on my cheeks like tears falling of their own volition,
the evening news shows me a Somali man kneeling
frostbitten, and parents rubbing their baby's tiny toes,
all finding refuge first in Emerson, Manitoba, then
in Winnipeg, having fled America, of all places
with its Emma Lazarus scripture, to arrive in the dark
like dreams, or confessions rising from the unconscious
guilt of a nation. Today in Winnipeg it is minus 20°,
so cold you might wish to die when the wind blows,
where my mother was born in 1912, her refugee mother
giving birth to her alone on the farm, her refugee father
waiting to register her birth until May when he was
going to town anyway. Today, Winnipeg's Salvation
Army is setting up beds in spare rooms, just as my mother
would have done for *mishpocha* from Canada after
she became American. Beyond the Bardo now, my mother
is so fused in my memory with Winnipeg that it seems
to me our refugees are running toward my mother.

Charlene Fix is the author of *Flowering Bruno* (poems, XOXOX Press 2006, *Mischief* (poems, Pudding House Press 2003), *Charlene Fix: Greatest Hits* (poems, Kattywompus Press 2012), *Harpo Marx as Trickster* (criticism, McFarland 2013), and *Frankenstein's Flowers,* (poems, CW Books 2014). She is an Emeritus Professor of English at Columbus College of Art and Design. Charlene co-coordinates Hospital Poets, part of the Ohio State University Medicine and the Arts initiative, and is an activist for Middle East peace. She is seeking a home for three manuscripts of poems.

Pocahontas Warren - February 11
Geoffry Smalley

Guadalupe Rodriguez*

Men Like You

Growing up, my momma always told me
I was the key to their dreams
I never understood what she meant
I remember my momma would come home from work
With chapped, bleeding hands
Thorns stuck in her palms
My momma would miss bedtimes
Conferences, field trips, Student of the Month awards
To work for men like you
My daddy missed my birth
To work for men like you
I'm the first child
Born on U.S. soil to my illegal, Hispanic parents
My older brother and sister would tell me
That I would go far in life and
Make my family proud
Now I know why
They would put so much pressure on me
My momma told me about the day
She decided to leave her *Tierra Linda*
As she called her Guanajuato, Mexico
To escape poverty
To give my brother and sister
A brighter future
And the chance for an education
My momma was 18 years old
With a four-year-old and a two-year-old
She left all she had ever known
So her children could stop starving
She traveled in the back of a truck
With my brother and sister
And 10 strangers
To chase *el sueño Americano*
They rode for days without stopping
'Til they got to a desert where they walked for miles
My momma told me about the hot days
And cold nights she spent on that desert
At one point she had to sleep
In her bra and underwear
She wrapped her children in her own clothes

To keep them warm
The temperatures were brutal
Not everybody made it
My momma told me about crossing
El Rio Grande with my sister in her arms
And my brother on her back
The current was vicious
My momma never let go of my sister
But my brother got lost in the water
My mother got my sister to safety
And went back to look for my brother
She pulled him from the water
And lay him on the ground
His eyes were closed
She pressed on his stomach
Blew air in his mouth
And tried not to lose hope
At the 3rd try, he gasped
And coughed out water
They had come too far to give up
Got to the border
The bright moon
Was the only light they had to guide them
There was a hole at the very bottom of the border fence

Their feet touched American soil
My momma was 18 years old
The day she last saw her own mother
She's 45 now
She hopes that one day she will get to hold my grandmother again
That she won't be just another voice on the phone
That she won't die
Without seeing her mother
One last time
Her dream is that her own daughter
Will not have to spend *her* whole life
Working for men like you

I Love

I love my illegal immigrants
I love us because everyday
We wake to a country that hates us
We wake up, give thanks to God
And go to work
We come home and watch the news
Hear our own tv's deem us criminals
We change the channel
And pray that tomorrow will be a better day
When they give us a little breathing room
Like DACA we make the most of it
We are so grateful
That often we forget we deserve better
We stay low on the radar
Because we want peace
Want to exist without the added stress
Of having to be public
About where our spirits ache

We just want to work to feed our families
And yet we become scapegoats
To a system that is addicted to exploiting the poor
I love my illegal immigrants
Because the way our spirits are toyed with
You need some unfathomable strength
I love my illegal immigrants
Because we constantly
Have to prove our humanity
And we have constantly
Done it gracefully
I love my illegal immigrants
Because the hate Americans have for us
Will never be forced into my people's beautiful souls
Because to stay human under these conditions
You have to have an understanding of beauty

I love us even when our stories
Are manipulated and exploited
I love us because at the end of the day
Somehow we always manage
To make something out of nothing

There is nothing beautiful about being illegal
Nothing at all
But my people help me know
That no matter how this country
Tries to break us
I know strength and I strive
Thanks to my illegal immigrants

A pseudonym to protect her family

Guadalupe Rodriguez is 17, a high school student, and the mother of a one-year-old daughter. She has chosen to use a pseudonym as she and her daughter are the only members of her family legally allowed to be in this country. She fears for the safety of her parents, siblings, her partner and his family.

Reunió Para Trabajo

Mustered beneath the street lamp
in the dim before dawn,
el amanecer, they wait

for orders. Spanish rises
in tobacco smoke. Feet stamp.
The truck is late. *Policia*

were here *ayer*. Yesterday.
We're safe for now. No. Rumors.
Defundir los rumores.

Fewer than yesterday. Here.
Waiting. Where's Giancarlo?
Do you think? Ramondo

says it's ICE. Do you think?
Line up, line up, *formar fila,
formar fila*. It's coming.

El transporte. La camioneta.
To the warehouses. Let us
go work in the warehouses.

Hank Kalet is a poet and journalist from New Jersey. His work has appeared in regional and national publications, including The Progressive, In These Times, the Journal of New Jersey Poets, Big Hammer, Big Scream, The Free Press, and elsewhere. His latest book, *As an Alien in a Land of Promise*, was published in 2016 and is a hybrid work of poetry, journalism and photography.

Emigration

My best friend, R, once told me
her pregnant mother hid in the near
suffocating heat of a semi's engine
compartment to cross the Mexican border,

so she could be born a citizen,
economic refugees chasing a dream,
much like those faceless fruit-names
hanging from my own family tree.

But now, a small man has his orange hands
up Lady Liberty's copper green dress,
while he blows out her symbolic torch,
smothering the fires in her own eyes.

But now, her arms shake with PTSD anxiety,
no longer open to fold to her mother's breast
the hungry, the poor, the masses yearning to be free.

Now, she whispers names to ICE,
sings them on the New York salt breeze,
accompanied by a six-string acoustic guitar
as Burl Ives once sang to Joe McCarthy.

Now, refugees fear the knock on the door,
live by muffled voices and candlelight
huddled in ghetto basements, ever listening
for bootsteps on the floorboards.

They flee their promised land, this country
of opportunity, risking arrest and deportation,
or worse. Now, their frostbitten fingers fight
through snowbanks that wall our kinder border.

R says she still hunts the dream along pockmarked
train tracks nailed to an ebbing sand tide,
this single mother, her forty hour work week,
her evening classes. She says when she wakes in the dark,

when sleep is scarce and early morning shadows
amplify the imagination, she listens for the bootsteps
on the floorboards, and swears she hears the knock.

Nathan Tompkins is a writer living in Portland, though his heart will always be in north Idaho. His work has appeared in many publications including Menacing Hedge, Full of Crow, and Drunk Monkeys. He's the author of four chapbooks, most recently *Lullabies to a Whiskey Bottle* and *A Song of Chaos*.

Jane Mead

World of Made and Unmade
—Excerpts from the book-length poem

In the hills above Rincon
a woman is leaving jugs of fresh water
outside the Rincon Water Works

before locking the metal doors.

Rincon, where the Rio Grande
turns back on itself—
like the crook of an arm

before heading south to become
Rio Bravo del Norte. Rincon, a stop
for water on the journey north.

> ★

In animal darkness, before
the first day of harvest,
I walk up the vineyard's main avenue—

thumbnail moon, and the floodlight
from the big barn. Clanks and shouts.

The squat stone structures of the homestead
vanish, its layers of ghosts flicker
and go out. The black dog Leo follows me—

almost invisible when I look back:
he floats—a low-lying, uncomplaining
black cloud. *Day by day,* I hum—

to the dog and the moon and the vineyard,
I guess—*Let me see you more clearly.*

Love is a ticket, whatever love is.
And to where I could not say.

> ★

This year I have disappeared
from the harvest routine—

the pickers throwing their trays
under the vines, grape hooks
flying, the heavy bunches flying—

pickers running to the running tractors
with trays held high above their heads
and the arc of dark fruit

falling heavily into the half-ton bins.

The hornets swarming in the diesel-filled air.

★

The hornets swarm in the diesel-filled air.

Wagons of grapes bump along
behind the tractor, the tractor
speeds to the concrete loading slab.

Joel backs and fills, slowly places
each bin on the truck with intense
precision—the makeshift tines

of our "forklift" slipped
onto the bucket of the backhoe.

From my mother's cabin I hear
the exhausted crews come in,
stream down the vineyard road—

their shouts distant and nearing.
And when they pass the cabin—
Viva los Estados Unidos.

★

From my mother's cabin I hear them—
Viva los Estados Unidos.

This year I haven't picked figs
or taken them sun-warm to the barn

or left them in the big tin bowl
where the flags of the US and Mexico
hang high in the rafters, left them

with the little sign: *Viva Mexico*—.

This year—

I haven't balanced on the wagon
picking bad fruit from the two bins,

or walked behind the pickers with my bucket,
or watched the bins being strapped
on the trucks, cinched down—

my white hands
fruit-sticky at my sides.

This year
I have disappeared.

Or I was never there.
Or I was never here.

     ★

Mexico is a snake eating
its tail, Mexico—the fathers
shooting each other's sons, the sons

shooting each other's fathers, bodies
hung like flags from bridges,
as in the papers,

but not just in the papers—

home home home. The pastel
house on the river, salt cedar—
viva viva viva. Mexico

is a house on fire.

Miedo en todas partes.
Fear everywhere.

★

When this is all over
Ramon and Silvia say

we will take you to visit our home.

One day, they say, *we will take you
to Michoacan, from where we come.*

★

Somewhere in New Mexico
the house that is always cracking
continues to crack.—

Somewhere in Mexico a father
pays half the ransom and gets
half his daughter's body back.

★

How will you spend your courage,
Her life asks my life.

*No courage spent of
bloodshot/gunshot/taproot/eye—*

How will you make your way?

Then, *respond to the day
some other way than blind—*

★

The United States of America
Does not extend refugee status

To Mexicans.

★

And the bit about the answer
blowing in the wind—
what does it mean?

As a flag blows?
A leaf downed? A leaf hanging?
Or like a piece of grit
when the last thing in the world you need
is grit in the eye?

      ★

Because elsewhere in this valley
working in an orchard is the man
from Mexico—who on the eve

of his daughter's quinceañera
was able to pay only half her ransom.

Can no amount of squinting bring this
into full view of the life-size heart?

      ★

Rincon, where the Rio Grande turns
back on itself before heading south
to become Rio Bravo del Norte. Rincon,

a stop on the long journey to The North—-
where demand for water runs so high
that by the time it reaches Mexico

the river sometimes runs dry.

Jane Mead is the author of five collections of poetry, most recently *World of Made and Unmade* (Alice James, 2016). She's the recipient of a Guggenheim Foundation Fellowship, a Whiting Writers Award, and a Lannan Foundation Completion Grant. For many years Poet-in-Residence at Wake Forest University, she manages her family's ranch in northern California. She has taught as a visiting writer at Washington University, Colby College and most recently, The University of Iowa.

A Resident at Isabella Towers
Knoxville, TN 11/8/2016

has abandoned
her embroidery

     up late corralling
     her short temper

her dinner uneaten
gone cold hours ago

     tuned to CNN
     she witnessed a country

unraveling
in all likelihood

     from whatever
     the headlines will blame

in tomorrow's
morning news

        ★

     well past her bedtime
     she gains the wherewithal

to experiment
with nuanced expressions

     I need my fuckitol pills
     for example

as she knows
the days

     the weeks
     will move forward

with perspectives
imploding

        as what seems miraculous
        to some is quite

the American horror story
to others

               ★

O America
why does she tick off

        the innumerable
        variations on

land of the free
to mean this country

        embattled by its traditions
        of yin versus yang

the hodgepodge
& the same–same

        O America
        why must she call it

quits before the final tally
& cast herself to bed

        sweeping aside &
        into the air

the forgotten stack
of handkerchiefs

embroidered but
half-complete

        partially considered
        false starts

intended to be
artful keepsakes

      that scatter the floor
      like white flags

of surrender
as though she is undecided

      whether to stitch
      a pachyderm or jackass

from personal conviction
or consensus

      of her countrymen

Darius Stewart holds an MFA from the Michener Center for Writers, where he was a James A. Michener Fellow in poetry. He is author of the poetry chapbook collections: *The Terribly Beautiful* (2006) and *Sotto Voce* (2008), each an Editor's Choice Selection in the Main Street Rag Poetry Chapbook Series, and *The Ghost the Night Becomes* (2014), winner of the 2013 Gertrude Press Poetry Chapbook Competition. Other poems and creative nonfiction prose are published in Appalachian Heritage, Callaloo, Meridian, Chelsea Station Magazine, the Good Men Project, storySouth, the Best Gay Poetry 2008, the Southern Poetry Anthology (volumes III and VI), the Potomac Review, Verse Daily and numerous others. He presently tends bar at an award-winning seafood house in Knoxville, TN, where he lives somewhat comfortably with his dog, Fry. In Fall 2017, he will begin the MFA program in Creative Nonfiction at the University of Iowa.

Brittany Adames

Static

Mami sips black coffee in the morning,
crushes hardened bread between portly fingers

as news crumbles in a noiseless heap like
the t-shirts speckled in dirt stains in the room next door.

Silence soaked not only into her skin,
but into her tongue.

She lightly wades among heavily-accented "good mornings,"
soft blush scorching skin and branding her alien.

Papi sits on the dining chair,
its left leg unstabilized under heavy weight.

Thin t-shirt sticks to brown skin and
the only things he is fixated on are

the broken seams of an American canvas.
His image of red, white, and blue are singed

at the corners in blots of scarlet.
He casts his gaze downward,

callouses appear coarse and ash-stricken
like only an immigrant's would.

There is no November 8 in this household,
only tongues lodged against the rifts of our gums,

only English phonetics that are nothing
but fleeting among rolled r's.

There is no November 8 in this household,
only flecks of ire in the gaze of two brown children,

only the broad shoulders of those who
hoist that white woman's look of revulsion

at the sound of the language that is not hers
in a land that is not hers either.

The morning is dank and hollow;
we pour ourselves into the concrete,

blood-sodden in fervid prayer.
Paper documents with folded edges

scatter the yellow-brown table.
Small print says this is home, the land of the free.

Papi flits his gaze downcast once more
and feels his heart nestled in the pit of his stomach.

America is beautiful,
but only for those whose callouses are smooth.

Brittany Adames is an eighteen-year-old Dominican-American writer from eastern Pennsylvania. She spends most of her time writing poetry and leaving short stories half-finished. She has been regionally and nationally recognized by the Scholastic Writing Awards and is an alumna of Susquehanna University's Advanced Writers Workshop and Kenyon College's Writers Workshop. She has been featured in the publications such as Calamity Magazine. She is currently a writer for Affinity Magazine, Glue Magazine, and Women's Republic. Her favorite word is resistance.

Thank you, Tennessee

I am lucky   I am told
To have a job.

I must choose
        between my mortgage
and paying for the endoscopy
        for my eight-year old.

This is the American dream:
Living paycheck to
        three days before paycheck
scrounging in sofa cushions
        counting change in terms of bread
        slices, miles driven, hours of air
        conditioning.

Keri Withington is passionate about studying social issues and advocating for social equity. Professionally, she is an educator and author based in the shadow of the Smoky Mountains. Her work has previously appeared in numerous journals and anthologies, recently including Blue Fifth Review, Feminine Inq., and Calamus Journal.

Medicaid Waiver

/med-i-caid waiv-er/

omen

1. She comes to the door knock, hunched owl eyes and holds up a brown finger, *wait a minute*, it says. We wait in porch sun, sweating, rocking heels to toes, heels to toe. She opens the screen again, invites us into her dark room of two wood chairs, leather recliner, fish tank, stacks of unpacked moving boxes, the tired buzz of a fan looping in the dark above our heads. Visitors, we ask personal questions, about her health, her family's health, her struggles with health. We give her phone numbers, pamphlets, ask her to sign petitions. I record her story, reaching my arm out towards her as she starts crying to capture her flooding words of abuse, eye surgeries, diabetes, minimum wage, children on drugs, children without coverage, social security, cold houses, bad knees. The silver mic of the recorder glints off a hallway light and blinds me. My arm never reaches to touch her.
2. His eyes are rheumy and yellow, a faded mucus color like the tennis ball on the end of his cane. I ask if he would like to sit, and he waddles to turn the oven off, pauses his chicken wings and french fries. Back on the porch in a silver chair he is sweating. He has not eaten in two days. He has not left Ohio Street in 20 years, since the fall off the roof, since the seizures started. Sometimes he plays dominoes with the neighbor across the street. It keeps his mind sharp. Sometimes he visits his mother, nearing 93, healthier than him, healthier than his 14 siblings. What if the Republicans take away your health care coverage? Well, he says, I'd probably just kill myself.
3. Proposed Medicaid Waiver: If you do not work or volunteer 20 hours a week, you could lose your coverage; if you do not re-enroll every year, you could lose your coverage; if you miss an appointment, you could lose your coverage; if you do not make a monthly payment, you could be locked out of your coverage for six months, and then still have to pay for those six months; based on your income and family size, you will pay additional premiums and co-pays while losing access to vision, dental, hearing and emergency care.
4. The human body has tangible shapes, illnesses, inadequacies, injuries, injustices, and still we tell it, do better do better do better, you do not deserve its support, its systems, its cyclical breath, unless you do better.
5.

Austyn Gaffney is a writer based in Kentucky. She writes primarily non-fiction and her themes include social justice, environmental ethics, and travel. A version of this story can be heard on the podcast Power to the People produced by Kentuckians for the Commonwealth.

Walk With Me

I

Across the field at evening sun
I met him, heard his record
Of hatred; I wanted to run
The path back home, let discord
For separate races play on,
Out of my sight: Men in outfits,
White with little holes for scaring ones
Whose right to live in peace is lit
Forever; consider these, born
Little babies in arms of mothers
And fathers; those babes, grown, spinning
Their shame to tease others
To views rampant
With a child's impressionable
Mind to chance
A play uncomfortable.

The man's days spent in working—
Hard, he takes to drinking
Cans of beer by the case; the thirst
Drives him to non-stop thinking
How to spread *White*, denying
Being's many colors;
Believing that, belying
Times—even in darkest hours.
He would practice hate.
He would plow his corn, hoe beans
In comfort and promise no day
Would come to see him drunk and lean
From beer into bigotry
To take his life just
As if his John Deere could crush any sacredness
Of his mind and still accept a wider world
Than his small farm could,
Including visions of those who came to America as slaves.
Folly kept
Him focused on the Klan.
Perhaps it gave him a sense of being.

Disesteem ran
His world with slurs he'd spout toward me.

II

A shackled history
Can turn bricked-up misery
Into negatives begetting evil,
So that the heart's
Safeway to civil
Rest may spark
Lies, scattered, not much sense
Remaining, if one wants to know,
For example, that July, the slave girl, washed and rinsed
Clothes, walked around the lowgrounds of this man's ancestors,
And down rows in the Gnat Field,
Picking up points the Indians left
Before the Trail of Tears would yield
Sacrifices humans left bereft.

My Paul's Hill is just a place,
An original land-grant from King George: What chill
The first Stephenson who came
To settle and farm the fields
Must have felt when July's ancestors and descendants,
Their dreams
Put off, just about lost their chance,
The overseer little granting,
Since landlord and tenancy set recognition's
Proper treatment for races, planted
Here to work for decades in sized-up
Restraints formed by somebody else.
I started to say I
Have seen the black and white of belts
Swung against flesh to deny
People from fulfilling something
Inside that wants out,
To live in flinging
Harmony, away from the run
To hell and back to make
A Ku Klux Klan record turn on
A spindle what I shake to say
I heard, once, after a walk at setting sun.

Shelby Stephenson is Poet Laureate of North Carolina. Recent books: *Elegies for Small Game* (Press 53), winner of Roanoke-Chowan Award; *Family Matters: Homage to July, the Slave Girl* (Bellday Books), the Bellday Prize. A Distinguished Alumnus of the English Department, University of Wisconsin-Madison, he is Professor Emeritus, University of North Carolina-Pembroke, serving as editor of *Pembroke Magazine* from 1979 until his retirement in 2010. He lives at the homeplace on Paul's Hill, where he was born, near McGee's Crossroads, about ten miles north of Benson.

Luis Lopez-Maldonado

Thinking About Eating Real Mexican Food From A Real Fucking *Taqueria*, Not Some Fake Ass Shit Here In South Bend, IN

Monarca mariposa has yet to flutter here in sad white town, here where church and state fuck each other in the ass bareback bareback, here where Notre Dame™ drowns in gold gold crowns gold helmets gold napkins, here where fat kids have pink cheeks in winter and the only thing their parents know how to do is stick a T®ump sticker on their rusting rusting crusting cars—"Flour or corn tortillas?"

Luis Lopez–Maldonado is a Xicanx poeta, playwright, dancer, choreographer and educator, born and raised in Southern California. He earned a Bachelor of Arts degree from the University of California Riverside in Creative Writing and Dance. His poetry has been seen in The American Poetry Review, Foglifter, The Packinghouse Review, Public Pool, and Spillway, among many others. He also earned a Master of Arts degree in Dance from Florida State University, and a Master of Fine Arts degree in Creative Writing from the University of Notre Dame, where he was a poetry editorial assistant for the Notre Dame Review, founder of the men's writing workshop in the St. Joseph County Juvenile Justice Center, and the Recipient of the Sparks Summer Fellowship 2016. He is currently a co-founder and editor at *The Brillantina Project*. luislopez–maldonado.com

Wil Gibson

The spray-paint smile on the bridge is fake.
(a poem for Wynne, and all of eastern Arkansas; after C.L. Bledsoe)

There are bank parking lots full of
kids with Papaw's truck that is
covered in Confederate flags.
They drive up to Sonic and park
and drive back to the bank
to park again. They yell about
black people like dogs barking
after a pedestrian that has
never even come close to its yard.
They yip, and growl, and curl lips,
all full of tobacco spit and Daddy's
drunken rants and none of them
have ever seen an ocean. Never
thought to go see one. They don't
dream that big. There are bushels
of skeletons that block the street,
that block everyone from getting
out. There is a 90 year old matress
in Grandaddy's trailer that 3 family
members have died on. People have
fallen in love and hearts have been
broken all around that matress. There
are secrets behind the brick homes up
on the ridge and love in the trailer parks.
Across the street from the trailer park is
a middle school. Behind that middle school
is a spot under a tree where too many
locals have lost their virginity. There is still
blood on the ground in that spot. There are
houses with dirt floors and toothless women
at the kitchen table with bald, dying old men
out in the yard that yell in to the women at the
table. They say, *I Love ya, ya fat old bitch*, and
they mean every single word. They will not
understand what you mean, will look at you
like a confused dog when you tell them it is
disrespectful to call her that. There are problems
that rise from the greenish smoke, angry little people
who cook magic powders and choke the life out

of the bored locals. Everyone gags on
something. There are limits here, not only
on the signs. The speed leaks off the
3 bloated new downtown buildings
and drive thru liquor stores.
(THERE ARE DRIVE THRU LIQUOR STORES!)
Booze and the perception of movement
are the only options, but Little Rock
is scary and Forrest City is a big city
of 13,000 people if you could count
all the illegal farm workers. There are
drugs everywhere and nowhere and
all places in between. Evil hides in
quiet corners and in *only God can judge me*
smirks as it judges you from the front
church pew and tries to fight you in the
parking lot. There are issues unresolved
floating in the Walmart aisles where
shoppers mock each other after they
pass, always under their breath. No one
wants confrontation in such a holy place.
There are train tracks that still divide
the town along color lines. The whites
call the black side of town *Colored Town*
like their great-grandfathers did, and
hate those of us who ignore the
borders with a smile. There are places
that surround this little rice and cotton
cluster called *sundown towns*, where
they warn black people to get out by
sundown, and they do. There are
sundowns towns that warn white people
to get out by sundown, and they do.
(THERE ARE SUNDOWN TOWNS!)
There are rules here.
There are questions that
linger on tongues, but never
find the courage to come out
into the humid air, and dry
answers that no one seems to have
or want to share. Everyone knows
where McDonald's is, knows that
Hays and Wal-Mart switched spots,
that Burger King closed, and Sonic
crossed the street, but can't give you

directions to the library because
it closed last year, ain't it? The
willful ignorance soaks through
the street like a flood no one
cares about. They will drown someday.
No one wants to learn to swim.

Wil Gibson currently lives in Humboldt County, California where the trees are big. He has had five collections published by kind people, and has been included in a number of anthologies and lit mags both online and in print, such as Marsh Hawk Review, Button Poetry, Midwestern Gothic, Drunk in a Midnight Choir, Yellow Chair Review and more.

You can find links to books and more info at wilgibson.com

The Cracker Calling the Grits White

I applaud you helicopter mom.
I honor your righteous anger.
I've too have witnessed the post election
despair and the palpable sadness.

You deserve a participation trophy
for defending your little girl,
for insisting the heckling students
be expelled, for demanding
an escort service be created
on the spot, to guarantee her
safe passage to her dorm at night.

She will likely need therapy,
will suffer for years from PTSD
from the many micro aggressions,
the bullying, the jeers she faced
every time her t-shirt, hat
or bumper sticker yelled out
HILLARY SUCKS
BUT MONICA SWALLOWED
and MAKE THE WHITE HOUSE WHITE,
AGAIN.

The civil, mature and responsible thing
the "sore losers" and "cry babies" need to do
is to accept the final outcome and respect
the office of the president of the United States
just like you did back when…ohh, wait, riiight—

Frank X Walker, former Kentucky Poet Laureate, is a professor in the department of English and the African American and Africana Studies program at the University of Kentucky as well as the founding editor of PLUCK! The Journal of Affrilachian Arts & Culture. A Cave Canem Fellow and co-founder of the Affrilachian Poets, he is the author of eight collections of poetry including the recent *The Affrilachian Sonnets* and *Turn Me Loose: The Unghosting of Medgar Evers*. Voted one of the most creative professors in the south, he is the originator of the word, Affrilachia, and is dedicated to deconstructing and forcing a new definition of what it means to be Appalachian. The Lannan Poetry Fellowship Award recipient has degrees from the University of Kentucky and Spalding University as well as four honorary doctorates from the University of KY, Spalding University, Centre College and Transylvania University.

Nate Olison

A Post-Election Poem

white people still talking bout Dr. King like
they didn't bludgeon him with bricks
or snipe his life shut on a balcony
with a shot so perfect
his necktie flew off
before he hit the ground

I don't want to hear about peace
don't want it sending me postcards
from places I can't go

who died and made you dream?
who drink lead you to the water
the lake was so calm that night
it must've been holding its breath too
what genocide stopgap they peddling
this time?

my history is everywhere
still learning what to do with all of it

been searching for my better self
feel like maybe he's in the hood somewhere
growing fruit—you know
run off to go live in nurture

I been known what the score was
that gravity was incidental, just wrapping paper
for a world that could spin on just hate
dust—I believe evil is a pack of mouths
with no stomach to speak of
all the habits of teeth
without even the concept of enough

I ain't got no god
I still see god every day

I see my people scratching at hope
like a phantom limb

I have *so many* people
probably entirely too many
to save

today is a deep breath
today is the treasure trove
our children have taught me
about patience
the hard-fought mindfulness required
to piece together these jigsaw futures

today we solve the puzzle of self love
today is the day we don't feel the need to act
as if what hurts us don't hurt us

today is the day it don't hurt us.
today is the day we sic our resilience
on the hounds

the day we move sure-footed
in our best light, may we act intentionally
and not just with good intentions

may we hold each other close *and* accountable,
for each of us to arrive
healthy and courageous at the work
that's been calling our names

Nate Olison is a writer, performer, and teaching artist living in Chicago, Illinois. He received a BA in Fiction Writing from Columbia College in 2012. He has been teaching and performing poetry in the city for 10 years. As a youth development specialist and prison abolitionist, he is dedicated to helping young people overcome obstacles presented by systemic oppression.

He's also a competitive video game player and aspiring comic book creator in his spare time.

So Out of Words

In a world where too many people
have their fingers on the triggers

of guns aimed directly at black people,
we have borne witness, time

and time again, to executions
filmed on tiny cameras—

Which allow us to see too much
Which allow us to see not enough.

Judge, jury, executioner—
It's due process in the suburbs

and the city streets, on winding
country roads and highways, sidewalks

in front of the convenience store,
where the streetlights don't shine

in the back corner of a parking lot,
on the playground, behind the fence

in a field near your children's school
on the street in front of your house.

This interminable spectacle
of black death playing on a loop

over and over again until
we become numb to something

that is now a permanent part
of the American memory.

How could these grainy videos
not translate into justice?

I just don't know how to believe
change is possible

when there is so much
evidence to the contrary.

I am so out of words
in the face of such brutality.

Black lives matter, and then
in an instant, they don't.

(This poem is inspired by Roxanne Gay's editorial "When Black Lives Stop
Mattering", The New York Times 7/16/16)

Marjory Wentworth's most recent book of poetry is *New and Selected Poems.* She co-authored *Out of Wonder, Poems Praising Poets, Taking a Stand, The Evolution of Human Rights;* and *We Are Charleston, Tragedy and Triumph at Mother Emanuel.* And she is the author of the children's story *Shackles.* Marjory is on the faculty at The Art Institute of Charleston. She serves on the editorial board of the USC's Palmetto Poetry Series, and she is the poetry editor for *Charleston Currents.* Her work is included in the SC Poetry Archives at Furman University, and she is the Poet Laureate of South Carolina.

Into the Light

In light rain and gray skies, I wrote into the light.

I packed for the birds. I packed for the Northern Coastal Olympic Peninsula despite emptiness lodged in my stomach. I reached down to concrete before a hospital door. I reached down to retrieve a solitary ginkgo leaf. You do not have to be good to feel a tear to pull your breath in. It was November 10th 2016 when I opened my leather wallet and slid into place the yellow scalloped edges of hope. Two days later Kate Gray would publish her poem, Ginkgo Leaves. Hope was repeating itself. I began to breath.

Standing on the reservation in Neah Bay I opened my binocs to focus and felt the loss. I chose Barack first because he was black and behind you. When it came time for you I didn't ask what you needed. I didn't ask. I didn't ask if you were okay. All these years you have been a woman white in the trenches. You had my back. I thought I understood. I thought I had you. You didn't ask and I didn't know. How do I get you back? How do I say my sorrow is deep? They say complacency is striving for the Buddha. When all I feel is complacency lost the election.

Gulls are in flight of white to gray. Wingtips left to right. The distance between one thousand Eurasian Widgeons swimming the coastal shore and one thousand California Gulls in flight above is a ladder length. There is an eloquence of difference to be learned. I differentiate the female Eurasian Widgeon and the female Harlequin. As wheels of the van roll the Buddha asks only for emptiness. I consider the intellectual persuasion of the 60s. We are strong together never alone. We are powerful in voice in silence in muted notes. Drum. Bend boughs. We will stay. Call cach namc. Call my name.

From an election to a birding trip I missed understanding somehow the transition of the Northern Fulmar from salt water to fresh water. I'll return now to the Makah Tribe and a Cornell class.

In light rain and gray skies, I am hooded and pray to the light.

-Gail Alexander writes on a river in Vancouver, WA. This is her first publication.

Gregorio Gómez

Incandescent Free

Incandescent free, marching to a beat
Dancing songs of freedom, on the street
Pirates in the sunlight with gold teeth
The world is watching on bended knee
And the pipeline rumbles on standing rock, as Mr. Biggly procures his fee.

A world order has come to town,
It's looking to chop heads off women black and brown,
A hand upon a bible, fingers crossed
with a frown,
The 1%ers, yank the chain of the plebeians, upon the chair they crown a clown.

Tremors thunder, rock the seams of Mother Earth
While the insatiable avarice swine, distend their girth
In tuxedo tails and stove pipe hats, they parade their whores and their
        illegitimate births
Regurgitating fables, to the cheers of ghosts in white, tales from leaders
        filled with dearth.

A global warming eclipse, ice caps melting and a blood crimson moon
As midget urchins, devout sanguines, ejaculate their dirge, in an afternoon.
Across the universe, alternative facts are spewed like a crapshoot in
        a monsoon.
As the Batman's Penguin emerged from Gotham's murky waters, this one
        rises from its spittoon.

The festive mood of the new world order, with a million strong in contrast,
        is swiftly overshadowed.
From LA, Chitown, NYC, to Washington DC comes the salvo across the
        bow for the battle of the myriad of tomorrows.
Huitzilopochtli bright upon the sky, invigorates the fire in the belly. The cast
        has been forged in stone, for we shall not go the way of the Buffalo.

Gregorio Gómez, who emigrated from Veracruz, Mexico, is the MC of Chicago's most infamous and longest running underground Weeds Poetry Open Mic at the Hideout. For over three decades, Gómez has been a major influence in developing spoken word in many of Chicago's poetry venues. Gómez has been featured at many poetry venues throughout the Mid-West, and published in numerous alternative poetry magazines, including Stray Bullets Poetry Anthology published by Tia Chucha Press and the Poetry for Peace Anthology published by The Peace Museum of Chicago.

He is the owner/curator of SouthWorks '85 Gallery, and the writer, director, and producer of *Not Just Paintings on the Wall* documentary. He also produced *Blank Verse,* and *Israel in Exile*, two films by Juan Ramirez. Gómez is also the Executive Director of Latino Chicago Theater Company.

Now They Get It

That little boy they called
disobedient and crazy for
not pledging allegiance, ever
sent to the office often
prescribed him Ritalin
Now they get it

That little girl they called
disturbed and depressive for
cloaking as an Indian shaman with
ketchup all over her moccasins in
every Thanksgiving performance
prescribed her fluoxetine
Now they get it

That teenager they called
violent and full of internalized racism for
refusing to sing We Shall Overcome
every February in the school assemblies
put her in detention with MLK coloring books
Now they get it

Those protesters they called
unpatriotic and terrorists for
protesting the war in 2001
Stop & Frisk & Wall Street in 2012
Put them on that list, hacked and tracked

Those rappers they called
underground and out of touch for
never following trends for
never comin up off they M.C. stance
never smilin, always bout that Amerikkka's Most Wanted
never grinnin, always bout that Let The Rhythm Hit Em
never flawcin, always bout that Melle Mel, Beat Street
Now they get it

Them poets they called
not on the page and always rantin for
never writin or speakin bout that red wheelbarrow

never writin or speakin bout that rose that's still a rose
Cuz a white supremacist is a white supremacist is a white supremacist
is their president, again.

Malik Ameer Crumpler is a poet, rapper and music producer that's released several albums, short films and five books of poetry. He co-founded the literary journals: Madmens Calling, Visceral Brooklyn and Those That This. Malik has an MFA in Creative Writing from Long Island University, Brooklyn. He is the curator/host of Poets Live, Paris and the new editor-at-large for The Opiate. Crumpler also wrote several musicals, ballets/arias commissioned by Harvest Works, Liberation Dance Theater, Firehouse Space, Panoply Lab, B'AM Paris, B'AM Vancouver, and Double Wei Factory Hong Kong.

Incantation on the Eve of 2017

I turn bread into tortillas.
I leave dried guajillo chiles in my wake.
My hair is wild cilantro.
My footprints are poinsettias.
My tongue is an eagle whose wings will shout.
The fringe of my rebozo is made of infinite braids.
I dare you to touch.
I am a field.
My hands are dirt, my fingernails roots.
Diego Rivera has painted them.
My bones are made of corn and chiles.
My stomach is arroz con frijoles.
My lungs are comino y canela.
My blood is lemon and salt.
In my fingerprints are the spines of nopal.
Each one of my feet has six strings.
My steps are canciones, ground down cigars and ash.
La llorana leads my Mariachi band.
¡Toca la guitarra!
I paint streets the color of mangoes.
My face is all skull and a halo of carnations.
My elbows are molcajetes ready to grind and smash any fool
Who tries to build a wall around me.
Watch it crack like a tostada.
My shoulders are black doves.
My eyes are Ultima's owl, bless us.
It is my comal that will save.
Say my name!
Say La Raza!
We will sing until we raise hell.
¡Otra más!
As Emiliano Zapata chose to stand, we stand.
¡Vamos!
The statue of Liberty has stepped aside
for nuestra Señora de Guadalupe.
From Her robe falls no tears, only roses.
The crescent moon offers enough light for us to be on our feet
Among the stars,
Among the holy,
Among the mole.

We are America.
Our guitars, our tongues are aimed at you.
Loaded and heavy as fruit, ready to explode.

Footnote to Incantation of the Eve of 2017:

A *comal* is a cast iron griddle used for cooking and self defense. Poinsettias are native to Mexico.

The *eagle* comes from the Aztecs who founded *Tenochtitlan* with a vision of an eagle devouring a snake. I also have this image tattooed on my arm.

A *rebozo* is a Mexican shawl that is hand made and usually handed down.

Diego Rivera is a famous Mexican Muralist and philander who was lucky enough to be married to Frida Kahlo two times. Their first marriage was August 21, 1929. I was born on the same day fifty years later. I am lucky enough to live in Michigan where I may visit his *Detroit Industry* mural at the Detroit Institute of Arts.

Arroz con frijoles are rice and beans in various forms. They are beloved, nutritious, and a staple of Mexican cuisine.

Comino is cumin which is a common spice in almost all savory Mexican cooking (just a pinch). When I smell the tiniest scent of it, I am hungry.

Canela is Mexican cinnamon that is an ingredient in chocolate, mole, and can be used for the most delicious cup of tea.

Canciones are songs. Please sing your favorite.

La Llorana (the weeping woman) is a mythic figure in Mexico and America used to frighten little children from going out at night. It is only fitting that she should help us in all this darkness. She is not afraid.

Toca la guitarra (play your guitar) we need music and words to lead us.

I chose the color of *mangoes* because The House on Mango Street changed my life. Sandra Cisneros was the first Mexican American woman I read and then it was not until I was in high school. Her book made me feel less alone, for the first time. A million thanks to her work.

The skull and carnations are a straight up homage to *La Calavera Catrina*.

Molcajetes are a stone mortal and pestle used for making salsa, sauces, and perhaps a weapon if need be.

Black Doves serve two purposes, one is a shout out to Ana Castillo (another Mexican American badass writer) and the other is that it is one of my favorite songs, *Paloma Negra*. Go listen to it now.

Ultima is from Rudolfo Anaya's book <u>Bless Me, Ultima</u>. A book that made me want to walk around at day break in a black rebozo and look for owls, who would in turn, speak to me.

To stand up is from this Emiliano Zapata quote, "Prefiero morir de pie que vivir de rodillas."

Monica Rico is a second generation Mexican American feminist. Follow her at slowdownandeat.com.

AMERICA.ru

Newly Evolved Words for the Dictionary

noun **trumper;** a person who values showy but worthless things.
Derived **trumpery**; attractive with few needed qualities.
"From late Middle English denoting trickery:
from Old French *tromperie*, from *tromper* 'deceive."

sample sentence; I'd be a trumper, if I vote for trumpery.
Trumpery may have worth, but it has no value.

verb **trumpering;** practicing beliefs that are cursory, seductive,
delusive, shallow, twaddle, rubbish, nonsense or fallow.

adjective **trumpy;** "that trumpy hope which lets us dupe ourselves."

antonyms: integrity, common good, truth;
in order to have value, something must virtue all,
flash and common good must be integrated.

Source: oxford dictionaries.com, dictionaries.com, merriam-webster.com, Random House,
thesaurus, and my imagination.
Quote: E. M. Cioran

Lynn Geri waited until she was into her seventh decade to take up the study of poetry. She lives in Bellingham, WA and studies with David Wagoner.

Daniel M. Shapiro

"The Incredible Hulk Is Actually a Disaster"

The Orange Menace hates the Hulk most of all.
"Loser," he tells the cyber. "His lunchboxes
don't sell. Sad. I bought my son an action figure—
broke in minutes. And my son is no tough guy."

The Orange Menace says he can out-Hulk the Hulk.
He wants to go from calm to livid in under 6 seconds,
no need for pussified nostalgia to be a mortal again.
The color green can piss off—orange or gold only.

The Orange Menace flies to China for conversion therapy.
A doctor there can implant a chip in his brain that inhibits
all the shitty intimacy: smiles, handshakes, tender sex acts.
This doctor promises unlimited rage at the lowest of prices.

The Orange Menace wakes from surgery feeling peppy.
With thumbs the size of bread loaves, he begins to tweet
but presses 14 buttons at a time. He smashes his phone,
which only angers him more. He begins to cry violently.

The Orange Menace has not become a Hulk. Even the bigly
wears off, but not before he easily strangles his doctor
for using "a bitch chip instead of a manly chip." He returns
to normal size, buys a new phone, tweets: "@Hulk is weak."

"The Bigger the Crowd, the Bigger the Man"

The Orange Menace is not always tall.
He is listed as 6-foot-3, but that's his height
at full follower strength. During a dry spell—
nary a retweet—he can stay 3-foot-6 for days.

The Orange Menace lives in a gilded tower.
No one else knows about the 36th floor,
stocked with small suits and juice boxes.
When love stays grown, he won't need this.

The Orange Menace knows it's not the size
of a crowd that matters. Evil is a bankroll:
It's gigantic when people think it's gigantic.
The biggest, best safe can hide its emptiness.

The Orange Menace loves to hold rallies.
Today, he debuts The Duplicator, a gadget
that creates the illusion of twice as many.
He aims it at the crowd, feels taller than ever.

Daniel M. Shapiro is the author of *The Orange Menace* (locofo chaps, 2017), *Heavy Metal Fairy Tales* (Throwback Books, 2016), *How the Potato Chip Was Invented* (sunnyoutside press, 2013), and *The 44th-Worst Album Ever* (NAP Books, 2012). He is the senior poetry editor and reviews editor for Pittsburgh Poetry Review.

Narcissus In Chief - February 12
Geoffry Smalley

Jared Smith

Early November in an Election Year

In the mountains by our cabin
this early November the grasses are dry
pressed low against the ground but
they are not dead, are holding tomorrow
in their roots and in their seeds blowing
against our shutters, over the coffee rock
where we have spent 30 years of mornings
without radio or television hallucinations;
and though the breezes bitter toward winter
the elk are migrating up our old dirt road
to the high country and the bears sleep now
plump in their dens filled with tomorrow.
Moose are stripping the bark from aspens
because while nutrients are scarce there is water
and life still hidden in those things that grew
last year, and though the rabbits and foxes are prey
to the mountain lion tagged and set loose among us
a lion will take only some in such a vast land and time.

It is two days until election day in Washington
a long way away across the tarmac highways of America,
and the way this valley is angled with its long cascade of time
you can't see Cheyenne Mountain with its aerials and bunkers
nor the National Labs hunkered down in Boulder Valley
nor the satellites circling above us, nor can we see
whatever it is they see, but damn it all, we're at peace,
and we too are waiting for the spring.

Jared is the author of twelve volumes of poetry, with the 13th due out this summer. His work has appeared in hundreds of journals and anthologies in the US and abroad. He is the Poetry Editor of Turtle Island Quarterly, and has served on the editorial boards of The New York Quarterly, Home Planet News, The Pedestal Magazine, and Trail & Timberline, as well as on the boards of literary and arts non-profits in New York, Illinois, and Colorado. His website is jaredsmith.info

November, seeking light
   (after Lucille, missing Lucille)

1) Wednesday, November 9, 2016

Surprise and confusion and what began
in September 15 years ago
has become this dark November morn.

What God do we ask
to bless our country now?

2) Thursday, November 10

It is time to note the shadow inside
the skin we pretend to have shed,
the arrogance of good fortune.

It is time to look in the mirror
and see through to where the wiser owl
asks, "who   who   who?"

3) Friday, November 11

the language on the teleprompter
slides into history.

Still, feelings claw and cling
like ominous clouds with lightning bolts
and accusations thunderous as cannons.

4) Saturday, November 12

Shadows are drawn to shadows.
Our darker demons urge us
to watch the blood flow.

5) Sunday, November 13

The leaves continue to turn,
orange burning to red. They fall like rain,
dance in slow motion.
From the window it seems nothing has changed.
The natural world is unmoved.

I study all this with wonder

bear witness to our fragile humanity,
my silent fears.

6) Monday, November 14

The super moon illumines.
It is closer than it has been

closer than it will be,
like the seductive call of rage.

7) Tuesday, November 14

A week awash in paradox,
the confusions of politics and language.

What is spin?
What is genuine?

Does anyone remember
the sound of truth?

★★

Soon it will be Black Friday.
The stock market will have reached new highs.

It is always about money, isn't it?

In the algorithms of our Facebook universe,
in the safety of our gated communities,
we rarely see
those who are other.

What has become of us?
What have we become?

What must we do next?

Michael S. Glaser served as Poet Laureate of Maryland from 2004 – 2009. He is a Professor Emeritus at St. Mary's College of Maryland, a recipient of the Homer Dodge Endowed Award for Excellence in Teaching, the Columbia Merit Award for service to poetry, and Loyola College's Andrew White Medal for his dedication to the intellectual and scholarly life in Maryland. A member of the Board of Directors for Maryland Humanities, he has edited three anthologies of poetry, published several award winning volumes of his own work and most recently, co-edited the Complete Poems of Lucille Clifton for BOA Editions. More at michaelsglaser.com

Jane McPhetres Johnson

Growing Up Beside the Continental Divide

we lived on the eastern slope where the great slabs
of red stone tumbled down steep inclinations
above our heads and buried their sharp points
in the sandy soil where wild flower children followed
in the foothilly steps of Chief Left Hand's canyons

barely aware of the other side's western faces
except when we skied the highest mountain peaks
and got lured down "advanced-only" trails in error
or dare, ending somewhere over there where
great white mogul-ridden slopes tipped us over
and dumped us into summer fields of cantaloupes.

Who were these people anyway, staking out claims
to long straight rows of gain in their shiny tractor
cabs full of stereo talk-radio heads and cool A/C and
who were their followers, shadowy rows of fold-up
folks strung out behind, hands full of melons, eyes
peeled for another sort of slippery slope called ICE

and who are we in this country of pointless furs and
filtered glasses, one foot in salt of the earth-melting
fat cats' oil and gas pipes fracking our own mother's
bedrock and broken waters so we can keep the other
foot on the up slope, keep on truckin' and flying free
sky high over the not-so-ancient great wall of Mexico?

Dying out incontinentally divided now, hanged, drawn
and quartered into states of red and purple and black
and blue, so bruised and beaten down and swollen up
we've lost our heads and now we've got a head that's
lost his way, a bipolar chief for two polarized slopes
tottering, divided, forgetting how to lean on each other.

Jane McPhetres Johnson was born, raised, and educated on the eastern slope of the Colorado Rockies, migrated north to the Wyoming Big Horns, and recently landed on the eastern side of the Berkshire Hills in western Massachusetts. She completed the Goddard MFA under the care of Stephen Dobyns and Thomas Lux the same week her younger son was born, named him Ben Jo(h)nson, then dreamed up programming for public libraries until she finally got arrested at the George W. Bush White House and quit her library work to look for a more effective, affective voice. Always she has practiced the 3 Rs—Reading, wRiting, and Revision—but seldom has taken the next alphabetical leap to Submission. Recently, however, her poems are venturing out to become verbal expressions of the Munch-kin "Scream" in the face of militarism, exploitation, and the sad insanity of corporate lemmingism.

The People's Choice

I met a man without a core
who said, "I'll tell you what I'm for.
I'm for whatever I might say
that people want to hear today."

"But, Sir," I said, "that isn't right.
It isn't proper to recite
opinions that are not your own.
A man should stand by truth alone."

"By truth?" He laughed. "Your *truth's* a crock.
Here's truth," and he began to mock
the earnest souls who thought they knew
the things a man should say and do,

And people roared and howled with glee.
"They love *my* truth, and they love *me,*"
proclaimed the man without a core.
"Don't tell *me* what I should be for."

And people took him at his word—
which wasn't what they thought they heard—
and raised him high, and raised their voice:
"He's *Us!*" they cried. "The People's Choice!"

(May, 2016)

Bruce Bennett is the author of ten books of poetry and more than two dozen poetry chapbooks. His second *New And Selected Poems, Just Another Day in Just Our Town*, was published in January by Orchises Press.

His chapbook, *The Donald Trump of the Republic*, was published in May, 2016, by FootHills Publishing.

Choice

My ballot blocks my throat,
making it painful

to sing, speak, even cough.
I always thought

it would be enough. Now
the torn skin must

speak. The wet wound
must sing its protest.

We must find the streets
again, our human chants.

We must insist, with our throats
raw, our lips unsure.

Our neighbor-citizens
have eaten a rotten fruit.

We did not love them
out of it. We did not listen

with our hands. We did
not confront our deepest

sin when they spoke it.
We have swallowed

a page from a discredited
book. A lie revealed

as a lie, hundreds of times
over. This page of fear,

this invitation to hate
our neighbors. These

words live now,
because somehow,

we chose them.

Joseph Ross is the author of three books of poetry: *Ache* (2017), *Gospel of Dust* (2013) and *Meeting Bone Man* (2012). His poems appear in many anthologies and journals. He won the 2012 Pratt Library/ Little Patuxent Review Poetry Prize. He teaches English and Creative Writing at Gonzaga College High School in Washington, D.C. and writes regularly at JosephRoss.net

Taking It Down

The season aches from so much well-
wishing, of candle flames dyspeptic,
groaning inside the glass walls

of their overscented
outhouses, on the laced
bed tables of suburban couples

arguing over manners, or schools,
or money. A string of cheap lights
swings on a house's chest

like the pendants of some cheap
necklace. Weakly lit by a hungover sky,
gray as solitude.

On the television, a new president.

Gregg Murray is Assistant Professor of English at Georgia State University and the editor of Muse /A Journal. He has poems in Caketrain, DIAGRAM, Carolina Quarterly, Pank, New South, Birmingham Poetry Review, and elsewhere. He is the author of *Ceviche*, from Spittoon Press. Gregg also writes for The Huffington Post, The Chattahoochee Review, Real Pants, ArtsATL, The Fanzine, KurzweilAI, and others. He holds a Ph.D. in English Literature from the University of Minnesota.

Post–Election Blues

The hopeless
among us

are now
us

M. G. Stephens is the author of nineteen books, including the recently published short poems in *Occam's Razor* (2015), as well as the critically-acclaimed novel *The Brooklyn Book of the Dead*; the award-winning essay collection *Green Dreams*; and the memoir *Lost in Seoul* (Random House, 1990). Recent work has appeared in Missouri Review, Ploughshares, Hollins Critic, Rain Taxi, Notre Dame Review, PN Review (UK), and Brooklyn Rail, which monthly serialized his boxing novel *Kid Coole* from May 2015 to June 2016.

Survival Practice

I know how to start a fire
how to build shelter from sticks and leaves
and how to make love after being raped
I know how to run a 10k
how to cook on an open fire with a steel grate
how to purify water
I know how to navigate the wood and city streets
how to ask a stranger for help
how to travel light
I know how to file taxes and fill out spreadsheets
how to survive in a world that values my spreadsheets more than
        my survival skills
values my livelihood more than my life
I know how to survive another comedy show where a body like
        mine is the punchline
how to survive another horror story where a body like mine is
        the boogie man
how to survive another news clip where a body like mine is just
        another freak in a body bag
I know how to administer intramuscular testosterone shots
how to talk someone down from suicide
how to hide pills from myself
I know how to act in a crisis
how to watch my back
how to cope when watching my back isn't enough
I know because I've had to learn
despite every way they say people like me are weak
we are practiced in the habit of surviving
I know we fought so good we made cliche the phrase "it gets better"
soon it will be worse than I have been alive to remember
but
I know queer culture was built from what AIDS left behind
we have survived before
we have survival practice

Jasper Wirtshafter is a spoken word poet from Athens Ohio, in the foothills of the Appalachian Mountains. Currently, he lives in the least terrible town in Indiana. He performed with F Word Performers, a queer feminist art collective, for four years. His work has been published in A Quiet Courage and Us for President.

Letters Between Two Women, One in the USA, One in Switzerland, Following the US Presidential Election of the Man Who Grabs Pussy & Lost the Popular Vote

From: "Renee E. D'Aoust"
To: "Beth Couture"
Subject: Letter from Renee
Date: Saturday, November 12, 2016 12:14 PM

<u>Lugano, Switzerland</u>

Dear Beth:

And so the US Electoral College elects the sexual assaulter in chief—Trump. I'm gutted. Devastated.

How are you feeling, my beloved friend? I think of you on the front lines, serving people, finishing your MSW. How can I support you better?

How does it feel in America?

This morning, Tube of Fur woke at five a.m., as she does, and she grunted. Last night, we walked our chestnut trail; it's called *Sentiero Eden*. Waddle up, waddle down. It is small comfort to me that Tootsie does not know how screwed we are. She has stayed close by me all week, as I get out of bed, to teach, to write, to go to physical therapy. Wednesday after the results were clear, my physical therapist (she's Dutch) said: "this affects everyone!"

This is global climate change. This is the normalization of racism, hate, sexism, climate change denial, the denial of responsibility we have to our brown & black & every color & LGBTQ sisters and brothers, the sham that I'm supposed to get along, the idea that I'm supposed to normalize the sexual assaulter in chief, the idea that I'm supposed to support a system of white supremacy in the country whose passport I carry. This is the normalization of excuses that favor fascism.

I say, white people, this is on you. Squarely. I'm a white woman. This is on me.

Our black and brown and LGBTQ brothers & sisters have been terrified to live in America. We have killed our First Peoples through genocide and called it assimilation. No more. I'm now terrified, too. I never wanted to leave

America to live in Switzerland. Now, I do not want to come back. Why? I don't feel safe. Know: I've been raped, sexually abused, harassed, stalked. A friend told me last summer that I did not understand domestic violence. And I wondered, "Have I done such a great job of normalizing my self? The violence in my past?" You see, 25 years ago when I spoke up, my extended family stopped talking to me. My mother's two sisters shunned my mother. My aunt told me I was "precocious" and "guilty of everything [HE] would do from now on, to any other girl" if I didn't report. Another abuser stalked me online for years. Another woman told me "I wanted it." Have I spoken of how my body is a locus of assault? Have I written about it? In obscure terms. I will now speak up. I am terrified of global climate change. Global climate change affects my body and the earth. But brown and black and LGBTQ bodies have been terrorized for years. So my fear is privileged; I am a white body. I am terrified that the sexual assaulter in chief has normalized ignorance, normalized grabbing pussies, normalized grabbing my pussy.

I have been practicing a potpourri of radical self-care that includes drinking too much coffee, eating too many Italian cookies, breaking up with Facebook so I can freak out on Twitter, and grabbing Tube of Fur to cuddle.

Kindness is my religion, being a doormat is not. My belief in kindness has meant I keep my mouth shut. As a white woman, it has been my privilege to keep my mouth shut. But when my brother killed himself, I swore I would not abide bullshit. I have not kept my pledge. IN IAN'S NAME: I WILL SPEAK UP.

Beth, please be my witness. I am terrified.

I'm so grateful for the readings you sent last time. Please continue to help me see my own blindness, to break down my privilege, to serve.

Give my love to Esteban, too. I send you love during a time of war.

Renée

Dear Renée,

The other night I dreamt about dying. In the dream, I was somehow certain that I was going to die, and I was so scared and so angry and sad. I kept saying I wasn't ready, I had so much left to do, I couldn't die. Not yet. It reminded me of when Ed and I talked about death, about the afterlife, and it hit me in such a powerful way that maybe there wasn't anything after this life. Maybe we really do just die and rot, and that's it. I have never been able to accept that idea. I don't believe in heaven or hell, but I've always believed that we don't just stop, that there must be something after this and we will be aware of it. I don't know if I believe this because I actually believe it, or if I'm just too scared to think about the alternative. In that conversation with Ed, and in the dream, I faced it. I allowed myself to think that maybe that's all there is—death and no longer being. And I sobbed like I have never sobbed. I couldn't stop. It felt like someone was tearing out my insides. That's what it feels like now, almost all the time. Like I am looking into the face of something too horrible to comprehend and I can't stop sobbing. Like I am seeing the possibility of death for the first time. And I'm not ready to. I'm not ready to look, but I have no choice. I'm not ready to face the possibility that this is all there is.

Esteban and I decided a few months ago that we wanted to have a baby. This was such a big decision for us. I don't think it was something I had ever allowed myself to imagine, because I am terrified of being a mother, of fucking the kid up, of raising a kid in such a scary world. Getting pregnant always felt like such a selfish thing. There are so many kids in the world who need parents, so few resources to go around, so little certainty that the world would be okay for the kid. But we decided that to have a kid, to make one ourselves, would be an act of hope.

The day after the election, I realized that I could not bring a child into Trump's America, that I no longer believed enough in the good in the world to get pregnant. I think about having a baby now, and it feels so cruel, so absolutely harmful, and I can't do it. I think Esteban could still do it even though he understands my feelings, but I can't. I don't have that much hope. And it breaks my fucking heart every time I think about it. It feels like death, and the grief is so big, so powerful that I don't know what to do with it at all. We are looking into adoption now, and that may be the most ethical decision anyway. Certainly we can love the child the same. But it hurts so much to think that we don't, *can't* have the same hope we used to, the hope we worked so hard to have.

I guess that's what I'm feeling most of all—hopeless. For the first time. I've always been, in spite of my depression and anger and fear, in spite of the reality I see as a social worker, an optimist. I have always believed that no matter how bad things are, they can and likely will get better. Not without a fight, of course, not without a hell of a lot of work, but they will get better. Things will be okay. I'm not sure I believe that anymore. I know the US is a country built on slavery, on genocide, on greed. It's a country that claims values it so often acts in direct opposition of. Trump really is no surprise. But the loudness of his bigotry, his fear mongering, his stupidity, still surprises me.

My sister got married a little over a year ago and is now afraid that her marriage will be nullified, that the woman she loves will no longer be seen by those in power as her family. My three black nephews now have even more to be afraid of when they walk down the streets, because of the violence Trump endorses and encourages in his supporters. I work with students who are afraid for their lives, the lives of their families, their futures. This isn't how it should be. And I'll fight for how it should be, for how it will one day be. Because there's no other choice. Right now I'm grieving, and I feel there's no other choice but that either. I'm so grateful you're with me in the fighting, in the grieving.

So much love to you, and please give my love to Daniele, to your sweet dad, to the Tube of Fur (who always gives me hope).

Beth

Beth Couture is the author of *Women Born with Fur* (Jaded Ibis Press). She received her Ph.D. in Creative Writing from the Center for Writers at the University of Southern Mississippi. She currently lives in Philadelphia and is completing a Master's degree in Social Work at Bryn Mawr College.

-and-

Renée E. D'Aoust's first book *Body of a Dancer* (Etruscan Press) was a ForeWord Reviews Book of the Year finalist. D'Aoust teaches online at North Idaho College and is the Managing Editor of Assay: A Journal of Nonfiction Studies. She lives in Switzerland. reneedaoust.com

Stella Reed

Not hand nor bird

nor shrubbery.
Not one good turn deserving another.
Not cats nor dogs in the rain,
but sleeping while lying and out of the bag,
and certainly killing for curiosity's sake.
Killing birds with stones. Two. One stone.
Not even a penny for your thoughts, even really good, bigly, best thoughts.
Not sliced bread either.
He's cast out our infants, yours, mine, with bathwater.
Squashed those infinite angels dancing on pins.
Wool pulling, salt graining, speak of the devil.
Not America, not great. Not again.
This will cost our arms and legs.

Stella Reed is from Santa Fe, NM. She is a teacher with the WingSpan Poetry Project bringing poetry classes to residents in domestic violence and homeless shelters in Santa Fe. You can find her poems in the Bellingham Review and the American Journal of Poetry among other literary journals. Stella is currently at work on a collaborative manuscript with two other poets—a feminist response to the 2016 election in epistle form from the personas of mythological women.

The 45Th President Of The United States Of America Showed Up While I Was Sleeping

The 45th President of the United States of America showed up while I was sleeping. He brought a sack of tacos. Inside of each taco was a dead bird. I dumped as much hot sauce on the dead birds as I could, but I couldn't eat them. The president smiled, his mouth full of feathers, bits of beak lodged in his teeth. He swallowed and said I took him for granted. I drank as much water as I could, but I still couldn't wash the taste of bird out of my mouth. I began to feel sick. The 45th President of the United States of America excused himself from the table and disappeared into the bathroom. When he came out I said, What's with all the birds? And the 45th President of the United States said, I like birds because you can fit so many in your mouth at once that it feels like you are an island with no inhabitants in an unnamed ocean on a planet that refuses to exist.

Grant Gerald Miller was born in Memphis, Tennessee. He is currently an MFA candidate at the University of Alabama and an assistant editor at Black Warrior Review. His work has appeared or is set to appear in various journals including Hobart, Qu Magazine, Pom Pom Lit, Necessary Fiction, and Nimrod.

Fear and Loathing in Trump's America

It's different being gay now than it was in, say, October. In October, the progress we'd made as a movement seemed relatively secure, and our view was set on how we might better secure our freedoms. Now whatever we've achieved feels fragile, and our energies are occupied with trying to prevent a slide backward. We have had to give up on the future in attempting to save the past.

It was both unsurprising and traumatic to learn on Monday about a pending executive order that would take away our basic rights, and though it was a relief to learn the next morning that that executive order would not be issued, the stir of vulnerability will not soon quiet down. Donald Trump was contemplating rescinding President Barack Obama's executive order granting protections to L.G.B.T.Q. Americans working for federal agencies. That Trump did not, that day, expose us to legal discrimination by our own government does not mitigate this Administration's dark view of those who deviate from its narrow definition of normality—white, U.S.-born, heterosexual, able-bodied, and Christian—which excludes the majority of Americans.

On Wednesday, The Nation published a draft of a new executive order that would allow anyone to enact prejudice against L.G.B.T.Q. people on the basis of personal religious beliefs. Many medical services, elder-care services, and disability services are administered through religious organizations that could refuse help to those of whom they disapprove. One in five of the four hundred thousand kids in foster care identifies as L.G.B.T.Q., and under the order, placement agencies would not be obliged to take care of them. The daily roller coaster of rights tenuously sustained or completely undermined is dizzying.

The problems surfaced before Trump took office. Following the election, in Sarasota, Florida, a seventy-five-year-old gay man was pulled from his car, assaulted, and told, "You know my new President says we can kill all you faggots now." In Austin, Texas, vandals spray-painted "DYKE," "TRUMP," and a swastika on the front door of a lesbian couple. In North Canton, Ohio, a lesbian couple who had lived in their home peacefully for years found their car door and hood defaced with the slur "DYKE." In Rochester, New York, gay-pride rainbow flags were torched as they hung from people's homes. In Bean Blossom, Indiana, vandals painted "HEIL TRUMP," "FAG CHURCH," and a swastika on the side of St. David's Episcopal, a church that had welcomed L.G.B.T.Q. congregants. A North Carolina couple received a chilling message on their windshield: "Can't wait until your 'marriage' is overturned by a real president. Gay families = burn in hell. #Trump2016." A similarly hateful note appeared on the car of a Burlington, Iowa, minister: "So father homo, how does it feel to have Trump as your president? At least he's got a set of balls. They'll put marriage back where God wants it and take your's away. America's gonna take care of your faggity ass."

All of this was in keeping with the publicly expressed views of the new Administration. During his tenure in Congress, Mike Pence, as head of the Republican Study Committee, supported a constitutional amendment against gay marriage, opposed the repeal of the military ban on openly gay soldiers, and averred that "societal collapse was always brought about following an advent of the deterioration of marriage and family," suggesting that gay families would operationalize such a disruption of the social order. He believed that being gay was a choice and said that keeping gays from marrying was simply "God's idea." He later proposed cutting funding for AIDS research and diverting the money to "ex-gay" therapy programs. As governor of Indiana, he championed and signed the anti-L.G.B.T.Q. Religious Restoration Freedom Act, which he softened only after considerable pressure from big business.

Trump himself opposes gay marriage, and has nominated Neil Gorsuch to the Supreme Court. In response, Lambda Legal has for the first time declared pre-hearing opposition to a nomination, announcing, "Judge Gorsuch's judicial record is hostile toward LGBT people and his nomination to the U.S. Supreme Court is unacceptable." Rea Carey, the executive director of the National LGBTQ Task Force (I serve on the board of the National LGBTQ Task Force Action Fund), observed that Trump "has been playing deeply harmful games with LGBTQ people's lives throughout his campaign and every single day of his days-old presidency. The problem for him is we are everywhere—so when he signs executive orders designed to demonize and dehumanize anyone— Muslims, women, refugees, people of color, immigrants—he is attacking us all. President Trump does not get bonus points for discriminating a little. Not on our watch, not in our name."

Even if Hillary Clinton had been elected, there would have remained work to be done. The endless fight for a trans-inclusive Employment Non-discrimination Act (ENDA) would have continued twenty-three years after it was first introduced in Congress. ENDA was designed to establish as national law a prohibition against firing people just because they are gay—as can still be done in twenty-nine states. L.G.B.T.Q. populations likewise sought housing protections, so as not to be ejected by landlords who objected to their sexual orientation.

Over all, the country has tolerated an increasingly tiered system, in which those with higher income and education who live in the liberal states have had adequate liberty while others have not. In that calculus, I was one of the lucky ones, but it is easy to mistake relative privilege for insulation against an onslaught. Like many other gay Americans, I have been thinking a lot about Germany in the early nineteen-thirties, when gays and Jews who were woven into the social élite thought it couldn't happen to them. I have also thought about my time in Kabul, fifteen years ago, when I pored over an Afghan friend's childhood photo album from the nineteen-sixties, with its images of women in miniskirts on the same streets that I had seen awash with burqas. I have thought, too, about the gradual dismantling of reproductive justice in this country, undermined a little further every year. We can never afford to be complacent; there is no such thing as security when it comes to human rights.

Emma Lazarus, who wrote the well-known poem inscribed on the pedestal of the Statue of Liberty, also wrote, "Until we are all free, we are none of us free." It's hard to bring out the confetti and balloons to celebrate the fact that one anti-gay executive order didn't get signed even as we watch people who endured the long and gruelling refugee process denied entry to the United States. Some of those people are gay, fleeing countries where their sexual orientation makes them murder targets.

When I was in Libya reporting for The New Yorker, I befriended a medical student named Hasan Agili. He is gay, and when gay people started being massacred in Tripoli, he fled to Beirut, where he had no legal status, and wrote to me in despair. We spent two years getting him refugee classification, first from the U.N. and then from the U.S. government. I was able to obtain the support of Senator Kirsten Gillibrand, and Hasan was admitted to the United States in June. One condition of his coming here was that he have a permanent residence for at least his first six months. By the time that six months was over, he had become a cherished member of our household. Having a Muslim immigrant living with us sends a message to the people we know, to our children, and even to ourselves that someone who has been called "other" can become not only familiar but also loved.

When I was away for a few days this summer, not long after Hasan arrived in New York, he sent me an e-mail one night about what had been for him an astonishing experience. He had been sitting on the front stoop when two men walked past, hand in hand. They stopped to kiss each other, then ambled on. In much of New York, such mundane intimacies happen all the time, but for Hasan, the men's lack of shame and fear came as a revelation. He wrote, "My heart was beating so fast, out of excitement or euphoria . . . I don't know." I felt so proud of my country and its casual liberalisms.

There is another, more intimate level at which L.G.B.T.Q. Americans experience the surge of prejudice. For those whose own families have treated them with ambivalent hostility, the upswing of hate crimes since the election recapitulates old experiences of rejection. While most people who share familiar characteristics across generations have a safe refuge among their families, gay

271

people often do not. Latino kids are not rejected by their parents for being Latino, nor most Muslims disowned by their parents for being Muslims, but those who are gay are often the target of their families' disapprobation or outright hostility. To have the power of the new Administration ranged against us conjures those formative years when those on whom we depended for protection expressed the most vicious prejudice.

During the height of the AIDS crisis, gay activism sprang from despair; during the Obama years, it reflected idealism; and now it is fueled by paralyzing anxiety. It's hard to live with what is going wrong right now without anticipating everything else that could go wrong shortly. There have been waves of anti-gay prejudice for centuries, of course. But one crucial difference now is that many of us have children. My husband and I have tried to explain to our children what is going on, but I would at the same time like to protect them from the reality that the people who now run the show would invalidate our kind of family. My life with my children seems non-threatening enough; it includes taking them to school, cooking dinner together on weekends, sitting through tennis matches and swim meets, helping with homework. Prejudice against an ordinariness that the movement has only so recently achieved feels newly shocking.

When I was twenty-three, I went with my parents to the Dachau concentration camp. There was a display of photographs, including many grotesque images showing emaciated prisoners in tattered stripes, mounds of discarded clothing, slave crews working on pointless exercises. I found my mother, who was not given to public displays of emotion, weeping quietly in front of a photo of a woman walking with a child whose hand she was holding. It was an innocent-looking picture, but it was captioned "On the way to the gas chambers." My mother felt dissociated from the prisoner photos, but in that one, she saw herself and me. My mother said, "That could have been us." We wondered what that mother had told her child about their destination. My children live in a world that suddenly requires a surrender of their innocence, as I try to explain why we may be less than other families in the eyes of the changing law. We are nowhere near a holocaust in the U.S., but amid the nationalistic frenzy of the past few weeks, I have found myself more than once wondering how to tell my son about the people who hate us, from whom I will be able to protect him only imperfectly.

Surrounded by friends, married with children, I nonetheless feel very alone when my government turns against me. I had told Hasan that it wasn't like that here. I had told my children that we were safe and lucky. I had told my husband that we would go on and on and on and on. Perhaps all of that will remain true, but perhaps it won't, and that is an adjustment that sears itself into our most mundane activities. No, in October, our family felt very different from how it feels now. We were an open landscape, but now we are a citadel.

Andrew Solomon is a writer and lecturer on psychology, politics, and the arts; winner of the National Book Award; and an activist in LGBT rights, mental health, and the arts.

Sanctuary Cities NOW
Pete Railand

Red Alert

for Sher Singh

Another day the government's
color-coded system for warning
the public saw red & in my home
town, Providence, a man,
supposed Arab &, also,
a Muslim, was dragged off a train
bound from Boston to his own
home town, in Virginia, through
a crowd who called him names,
threatened his life, spit on him.
Later, he was identified
as an Indian Sikh, his turban
clarified. But the Mayor still
denied that anything had gone
wrong, seeing how his ceremonial
dagger, called a Kirpan, one of the five
sacred symbols of Sikhism, exceeded
in length the local legal limit for knives
one could have on one's person. One
person can expose the true nature
of a whole city, a whole country, during
a red scare. Shop-keepers you liked
yesterday are looted today; your best
friend's family one night is herded up
without all of their belongings, their
load lightened even more at the end
of a long train ride. No one says
where they went. Soon their stuff
& even their house belongs to other
people, & everyone's been told to stay
vigilant, to stay alert, & alert means
seeing red, forgetting who used
to live here.

Rick Benjamin believes in ancient wisdom, like, say, a verse from the Tao de Ching that begins, "If you want to be a leader, let go of control." He also believes in circulating wisdom, daily and always through poetry. He is the former state poet laureate of Rhode Island (2012 - 2016), and has published three books of poetry—*Passing Love* (2010), *Floating World* (2013), and *Endless Distances* (2015). He believes deeply in resistance and resilience.

Shane is Right as Rain

"Shane, Shane is right as rain," Shane sang to himself as he drove north on Pennsylvania Route 74 from York. He saw dark clouds ahead. He was driving Grandpap's '74 Chevy C10 Stepside pickup truck listening to President Trump talk about how he was going to get all the Mexicans out of the country. The old truck only had an AM radio. That was fine with Shane. Trump was on WHP-AM. Really, he was on every station now.

"Shane is right as rain," he sang to the open windows on this April afternoon. All those Lib'ral bitches that made fun of him weren't laughing now. Trump was Making America Great Again and Shane was part of it. He was on his way to a Klan rally in Grantham. Christians can't be Lib'rals and they were going to march across the Messiah College campus and let them know what's what. Shane dropped out of York Area High School. Shane knew Trump would put all those college bitches in their place.

"Here's a Trigger Warning bitches!" he said as he patted the AR15 in the rack behind his head. He kept on singing. Shane called his AR15 an M4 because Shane should have been a soldier. He tried to enlist but they turned him down. The Jews made up the intelligence test he flunked and the bitches at the recruiting station said he needed to lose about 100 pounds. What did they know? He could shoot. He could fight.

The old six-cylinder engine clattered with knock from cheap gas and old age as Shane started up the first hill north of York. Ahead riding on the shoulder was a guy on a bicycle. "Faggots wear bike shorts," Shane said to himself. As he got near the bicyclist he swerved right hitting the rider on the shoulder with his mirror. Shane then laid on the air horn he installed himself and yelled "Faggot!" laughing as he drove away.

The bicyclist stayed upright, kept pedaling and gave Shane the finger. Shane flashed anger, but kept going. He rolled down the next hill. No traffic at all on Saturday morning. Shane smiled.

Just past the crest of the next long hill, Shane pulled off the road and parked well off the shoulder. He grabbed his rifle, slid his overall-clad form from the driver's seat and walked to a pine tree just past the crest of a hill. He dropped to the ground and wiggled his plus-size body under the tree. He settled down in the pine needles, his massive midsection puddling out on either side of his body. He could see well down the hill to the south. Shane turned the switch on the battlesight scope. The red dot inside the sight glowed faintly.

He watched as the lone bicyclist pedaled smoothly up the long hill. When the bike was 200 meters away Shane listened for traffic. Hearing none, he set the magazine on the patch of dirt he cleared in the pine-needle covered ground. Shane put his right cheek on the collapsible stock, put the red dot in the middle of rider's chest, flipped the safety to Fire and squeezed the trigger.

The rider collapsed on the handlebars. His legs wobbled. His right foot twisted out of the cleated pedal, but the left foot stayed locked in. The bike swerved left and fell. He was dead before he hit the ground. Shane rolled out from under the pine tree flipped the lever on his weapon to Safe and walked as quickly as he could back to Grandpap's C10.

"Shane is right as rain," the unemployed Trump supporter said softly and smiled as he returned the rifle to the rack in the rear window. "One round, one dead faggot," he said louder as he started the old truck. Shane looked left, signaled and drove down the hill and toward the Klan rally.

An ambulance sped past to the south. "Don't need no ambulance," said Shane as he watched the red lights blaze. "Bicycles don't belong on the damn road in Trump America," he said to his open window.

Twenty minutes later he pulled off the road near the Messiah College campus. Shane saw dozens of Klansmen with their hoods off looking at their phones. Shane grabbed his sheet and locked the door to the truck. He walked over to a group of men and heard one of them say, "Shot dead. A fucking General in the Army National Guard. The real fucking deal." Shane started to ask, then decided to just listen. Shane had no money for a smart-phone so he had no idea what they were talking about. After a few minutes it became clear that the "faggot" he shot was General Pete Stevens, one of the most Conservative Congressmen in America. Trump loved the guy. Pete was an Apache pilot. He fought in Iraq.

"Shit," Shane said to himself as he slipped away from the group and walked back toward his truck. "Ain't right a General should ride a bike. Ain't my fault." He climbed in his truck and stared at sheet-clad men staring at their phones on the field in front of him, tears in his eyes. He put the key in the ignition, then took it out again. *Cops won't come here*, he thought to himself.. *Best I just do what I came to do.*

Shane swung his legs left and slid from the seat. He pulled his hood so no one could see he had been crying. He walked back to the group as they lined up to march. "Shane is right as rain," he said to himself as he faded into the middle of the crowd of damp specters.

Neil Gussman enlisted near the end of the Viet Nam War in 1972. He served in the Cold War as a tank commander in Germany, left the Army in 1980 and started writing, mostly about chemistry and the history of chemistry. In 2007, at 54 years old, he re-enlisted in the Army National Guard and deployed to Iraq in 2009. Since re-enlisting, he has been writing about serving in the Army as a very old soldier at armynow.blogspot.com.

Watching the New First Lady

It's disheartening
the way patriarchal streams flow
to the sewers
bringing young wide eyed models
beauty queens and mail order brides
heralding gold-painted empowerment to the high towers and hallowed halls
superimposed on back alleys and trafficking in hopes of the poverty-fled
with opportunities reduced to
flat-ironed hair, stilettos and
narrowed eyes
stinging from the stench.

Her bare legs in temperate January make me chuckle
at oppressive white tears
streaming down shaven noses
bottled up in breast implants
offered up on a platter for
ravenous consumption of emboldened white mediocrity,

preening themselves.

She deserves more, so I donate my anger.

Because her tight weary smiles
don't matter to those who laud her appearance, three steps
behind his plan for our destruction
dulled into stupidity, stunted behind another language
and unfinished degree.

Their offensive excitement at this poor replacement of
the promise fulfilled – the daughter of force
calling forth fears
that bare arms attached to an exercised brain can be loved
by a man of the same
emotional capacity with deep perspicacity,

is dispiriting.

Their happiness bellowing cheers at her self-imposed captivity,
resonates loudly as the music celebrates a return

to the white man's true hopes and order of things

where her beauty,

if duly matched with subservience,

is the only reward.

Talia Lamoy is a West Indian with too many liberal opinions to live comfortably in her region. As a New York Matrimonial attorney, her compassion is often exhausted on her clients. She has been writing since she was in middle school, but is too sensitive about to her work to share all of it. With her long history of bitching about bullshit sexism, third world corruption, corporate mismanagement, racism, bad marriages and oppressive parents, no one would be surprised to learn she is a part of the resistance.

Ave, Mr. President

In our slow brook the handsome umber
leaf floats calm no matter
the vicious winds of a winter thaw.
My dark grandchildren wonder
at what they don't yet know to call
but I do *dignity.* Farewell.

–January 20, 2016

Sydney Lea was Poet Laureate of Vermont (2011-15). His twelfth collection of poems is *No Doubt the Nameless* (Four Way Books, NYC, 2016). His fourth collection of lyrical essays, *What's the Story? Short Takes on a Life Grown Long*, appeared in 2015. A former Pulitzer finalist and winner of the peer-reviewed Poets' Prize, Lea founded and for thirteen years edited New England Review. Before his retirement, he had taught at Dartmouth, Yale, Middlebury, Franklin College (Switzerland), Eotvos Lorand University (Budapest), and elsewhere. He has received fellowships from the Guggenheim, Fulbright, and Rockefeller Foundations, and his thirteenth book of poems, *Here*, will appear in 2018.

Sue Robin

My Entire Retirement Fund

The stock market is up
All those with money are ecstatic
Less regulations, less taxes
More money
Even my retirement fund is higher
But at what price?
People will be without care
The environment will suffer
Worldwide friendships will falter
All to make the rich-richer
I would give all my gains
Hell, I would give my entire retirement fund
To have clean water, air to fill my lungs,
Doctors to heal the sick and
Welcome mats instead of walls

— 2/28/17

Sue Robin retired in 2012 from a thirty-eight year career as a Marriage and Family Therapist. She has been keeping herself sane writing poetry for the last thirty-five years. Her son and grandchildren offer ample opportunities for joy and laughter.

James Schwartz

A Drop of Water

Land of lapping lakes,
Peninsula
&
Pine.
Alexis de Tocqueville,
Frontiersmen
&
Forefathers.
Detroit flood
&
Detroit debt
Our kingdom for a drop of water.

James Schwartz is a gay ex–Amish poet and slam performer. His poetry has been published by various poetry journals including Poetry 24, Babel, The New Verse News, Nostrovia! Poetry, piecejournal, Silver Birch Press blog and Eris Magazine. His book, *The Literary Party: Growing Up Gay and Amish in America*, was published by inGroup Press in 2011 and his poetry is anthologized in Among the Leaves: Queer Male Poets on the Midwestern Experience (2012), Milk and Honey Siren (2013), The Squire: Page-A-Day Poetry Anthology 2015, Writing Knights Press 2014 Anthology, QDA: A Queer Disability Anthology (2015), and various chap books, including Alpine Suite (2013), Poetry 4 Food 2 (2013), Poetry 4 Food 3 (2014), Arrival and Departure (2014), Secular, Satirical & Sacred Meditations (2016), Michigan Meditations (2016). He resides in Michigan.

Visit his site at Literaryparty.blogspot.com
and follow him on Twitter @queeraspoetry.

Thunderbird Woman
Isaac Murdoch

At Risk of Drowning

I love this road. Its metropolitan name, Fifth Street, belies its rural character. Just past the Rainbow Oaks—a favorite of truckers and bikers, which means good coffee, ample servings and a bar—acres of plants potted for sale line the road's borders. Rustic fences, never-mowed yards, overhanging trees. And it has a wonderful dip, to accommodate a creek that becomes a roiling river when we have the rare downpour in San Diego County.

After the dip, littered today with nature's refuse, is the shop where students stop in to buy tamarind and chili candies. Then there's the one-school district campus, still so waterlogged from the unusual days of rain, the kids are having recess in the county park next door. Some of the children are my eighth-grade students, most of whom want to go to college, so they allow me to teach them how to write, which I also love. My weekly visits to Rainbow, California are pretty sweet.

Not today, though.

Heading home from the writing class, mine is the only car on the road, but I don't appreciate the solitude, the familiar beauty, the remnants of a storm glistening in leaves turned to the sun. Instead, I'm grinding my teeth to yet another reminder of a hideous presidential campaign, a hateful first week in office, a regular barrage of ugly pronouncements; to the narcissistic rhythm of a Donald Trump and Theresa May press conference on the radio; to insipid declarations of the greatness of their new "special relationship."

If Trump weren't such a risk to the nation—to the world—the description's dissonance between today and when Winston Churchill first uttered it would be laughable.

But I'm not laughing when I notice the orange-vested men down the road by the dip and slow my car to an idle, although I'm grateful for the distraction from my grinding rage.

One man approaches with a labored gait—as though he's lugging something—but all he has is the SLOW-STOP sign dangling unused in his hand, flapping with the breeze of his movement.

He makes eye contact before I can turn off the radio and get my window down. His look is not bold, not scolding for some error I might have unintentionally committed. He's not smiling nor scowling. He looks... sad.

"It'll just be two or three minutes," he says. "You can wait here. If you want."

This is not the sort of traffic directing I'm used to.

"It's up to you," he says.

"I can go around the back way, no problem."

He looks at me.

"Or you can wait. It'll just be another two or three minutes."

He wants me to wait. He's sad and he wants me to wait.

"OK... How're you doing today?" I ask.

"Not so—We're conducting an investigation. It's, well, it's rough."

He looks at me, still.

I recall the local news, diminished by Trump's devastating executive orders. The storm-driven river rampaging through Rainbow. An older driver and a five-year-old boy. The days-long search.

"Oh," I say. "I'm so sorry."

"The boy didn't drown," the man says. "We found him in the brush. His little arms were wrapped around a tree. Waiting for someone to rescue him. Can't tell how long he'd been there. Just waiting. And a seventy-three-year old driver. Should've known better—with a five-year-old in the car. What was he thinking, trying to go through it?"

The man pauses, takes a weighted breath.

"We see a lot of dead bodies. Intoxicated, distracted, drowsy. All ages, but a lot of kids, teenage males speeding, kids texting. But that boy, holding onto the tree..."

His two-way radio sputters. The two or three minutes are up.

He looks at me, still.

Through the window, I take his hand.

"I'm sorry you have to do this," I say, "but thank you."

He lifts his eyes, glistening leaves turned to the sun.

I roll away from the man and reach for the radio, but I can't turn it on. I drive through the dip, under the trees, past the potted plants, the Rainbow Oaks, turn left on Old Highway 395, and pull over. I cry for the man, for the boy and the driver, for their families, for my nation at risk of drowning.

Kit-Bacon Gressitt, a founding editor of WritersResist.com, is a feminist writer and advocate for reproductive justice, immigration and LGBTQ rights. She also birthed a child of color, who's taught her a lot about white privilege and intersectionality. An erstwhile political columnist, K-B now has an MFA in Creative Writing, with an emphasis in narrative nonfiction.

The Day Trump Met May

The lady in red, in her kitten heels
Smiled as he confirmed their future trade deals
"We'll work it out together, both me and you
There really is life outside the EU."

"We will strengthen our special connection
And the world will see our unique affection
We can pride ourselves on our ethics and morals
We won't just sit back on our laurels."

"I am a people person, I think you are too
Let's show them all what we can do
The world can watch as we work things out
And Brexit's just great, I have no doubt."

"Brexit will be wonderful for your nation
And your people will forget their frustration
When they watch the new Maggie and Ron
And your days of uncertainty will be gone."

"I know that the UK's economically unsound
And leaving the EU, will weaken your pound
Negotiating from a position of weakness,
But I still love the UK and its uniqueness."

"I do support NATO, one hundred percent
But I still think too much money's been spent
And the distribution of costs really must change
I mean we're actually supporting Ukraine."

'I believe that torture, absolutely works
Discouraging evil from where it lurks.
We should all fight fire with fire
Otherwise the consequences will be dire."

"I love Mexico, and I love its folk
And I'm really a decent kind of bloke
But we'll continue to build our beautiful wall
Impenetrable, powerful and incredibly tall."

They then shook hands, by Churchill's bust
"It's only proper and fair and just
To reinstate it, in its rightful place,"
He said with a grin upon his face.

He then extended to her his hand
For all to see throughout the land,
The special relationship, so talked about
But the UK's media all started to shout,

"Has Theresa become Trump's Trojan horse
And is Britain's only real recourse
To listen to the words of a changeable man
Or is Theresa, Donald's most favourite fan?"

"You must come and visit our Queen,"
She said, as he agreed with a beam
"We must define our roles in the world."
And their fingers remained tightly curled.

Has Theresa reduced her bargaining power
Let's hope their relationship doesn't go sour
Or did she just want to be seen as nice
Maybe she did, but at what price?

"They'll be times we disagree," she fawned
He tucked his speech in his pocket and yawned
He was bored, this mercurial man
With his somewhat short, attention span.

Does Britain look desperate on the world stage
Or did we in fact manage to gauge
The measure of the White House's new resident
The leader of the free world's forty fifth president.

Cohl Warren-Howles lives in England and has a blog called Currently in Rhyme, where she covers events across the world, in rhyme. She has written a book entitled *The Silent Scream*, which is about ALS/MND.

Present happenings, in the nations of our time,
realist, idealist, she puts her thoughts in rhyme.
In this world of changes, that moves so very fast,
she tries and capture things before they have passed.

Her interests are varied, but just to name a few,
her words in her posts, will also give a clue.
She's a fan of Eckhart Tolle and the words of Mervyn Peake
and current world affairs, of which she will speak.

She loves stone circles and places in history,
The Law of Attraction and things of mystery,
she's a lover of images, especially black and white,
but it's the current world affairs, of which she writes.

currentlyinrhyme.wordpress.com
cawarrenhowles.com

Donald Trump

Change is the eternal law
With the passage of time.
The universal cult of the New World
Becomes in vain
For Trump like a bird of passage
Who wishes to replace the society
For the sake of Trump's rajya.

Trump's magic abolishes the tears of fears
Like the demonetization of Modi–magic.
Trump is a terror for all those
Who live in fool's paradise.

His master-stroke
Will breed the essence
Without fear of favor.

Arbind Kumar Choudhary, the originator of the Arbindonean Racy Style of versification and Indianised version of Arbindonean Sonnets in Indian English poetry, has propounded his philosophy of life, nature, love and poetry in *'Melody', 'Nature', 'Love',* and *'The Poet' for the saving grace of Tom, Dick and Harry on this strife-stricken earth.* Dr. Choudhary was included in the Cambridge Dictionary of English Writers, London in 2009, World Poetry Almanac, Mongolia in 2008, 2009 & 2010, Four Contemporary Indian English Poets, 2014, Romania, English Poetry in India, 2012, Contemporary Poets in 2012, World Poetry Yearbook, China, 2014, Five Indian English Poets, Jaipur, in 2015 and Twelve Contemporary Indian English Poets in 2016. Dr. A. K. Yadav edited two anthologies on his poems entitled, Arbindonean Iridescence in Indian English Poetry in 2015 and Arbindonean Luminosity in Indian English Poetry in 2016, published by Paradise Publishers, Jaipur. Presently Dr.Arbind Kumar Choudhary, an editor of Kohinoor, has been heading the Dept of English at Rangachahi College, Majuli, Assam, India.

The Trump Epigram

The fascist germ has recrudesced in the body
politic of America, so now America is sick
with hatred, fear, and "a passionate intensity"
for thinking a man with golden hair can make
it great again by building walls and towers.

It rose as a man through a crack in the minds
of his followers and energized the body
in the way a body jumps around before it falls
face-first to the ground and dies. Such a pretty
germ with a wide appeal to those who think
this fool is "fit" for the job. Such a siren song
that promises jobs in the hologram of his America.

So Mr. President, lover of Moloch, dealer
in Moloch, trader in Moloch, grabber of pussies
and tantrum tweeter, I speak to you directly
as a witness and silenced citizen, "I no longer
feel the ground beneath me." These are the words
of Osip Mandelstam to his executioner,
the "Kremlin Mountaineer" who also resembles
your apprentice, Vladimir. Forgive me Osip
for changing a word or two to address this germ

that's reappeared in America. Every despot
recrudesces the same as the last with a different
face but the same black heart. So boring as well
as depraved, or boring because depraved.

"Whenever there's a snatch of talk," you wrote,
in your cell, "it turns to the Kremlin Mountaineer."
So, God forbid we add the name, "Mar-a-Lago
Financier." In the meantime, you should know
that a "cloud of witnesses" is watching you.

Chard deNiord is the Poet Laureate of Vermont and author of six books of poetry, including *Interstate*, (The University of Pittsburgh Press, 2015), *The Double Truth* (University of Pittsburgh Press, 2011), *Night Mowing* (University of Pittsburgh Press, 2005), *Sharp Golden Thorn* (Marsh Hawk Press, 2003), *Speaking in Turn* (a collaboration with Tony Sanders), Gnomon Press, 2011, and *Asleep in the Fire* (University of Alabama Press, 1990). He teaches English and Creative Writing at Providence College, where he is a Professor of English. His book of essays and interviews with seven senior American poets (Galway Kinnell, Donald Hall. Maxine Kumin, Jack Gilbert, Ruth Stone, Lucille Clifton, Robert Bly) titled *Sad Friends, Drowned Lovers, Stapled Songs, Conversations and Reflections on 20th Century American Poets* was published by Marick Press in 2011. His poems have appeared in The Kenyon Review, Ploughshares, The Antioch Review, the American Poetry Review, The American Scholar, New Ohio Review, The New Republic, and The New York Times, Best American Poetry, and The Pushcart Prize. He is the co-founder and former program director of the New England College MFA Program in Poetry and a trustee of the Ruth Stone Trust. He lives in Westminster West, Vermont with his wife Liz.

Narcissus Redux

In his tower with his vodka and steaks
and the trappings of his for-profit pedagogical institution,
he fancies himself a kind of messiah, his mother was a
Gaelic madonna and while his old man could not
have conceived of this throne, this tower, his
middle name was Christ.

(*In the beginning, there were barracks and garden
apartments for U.S. Navy personnel.*)

He peers into pools asking, *What's on your mind?*
Forums, inboxes, chirping LCD screens, and Breitbart
reflect his assumptions. He sometimes leans in
until his nose is almost touching an interface, and
hundreds of thumbs float up to affirm him, the fat bird
replicates his 140-character sermons. His coif, his tangerine
ripples and wakes after almost every post.

But he's uneasy—

he's the son of man, the god-with-them, American as
the typeface emblazoning the *A* of his *Art*, Democratic as his
ghost-written *Deal*, but a few little eddies, some rills
at the edge of his visage are calling it wrong, calling it
cyber-malfeasance, a hack,
rubbing his synthetic gold ball and calling it   *.ru—*
calling him a proxy to a leaner, meaner man in Moscow.

Laura Page is a graduate of Southern Oregon University and editor in chief of Virga Magazine. Her work has appeared or is forthcoming in Rust + Moth, Crab Creek Reviw, Tinderbox Poetry Journal, HYPERTEXT, The Fanzine, Red Paint Hill, and others. She is the author of two chapbooks, *Children, Apostates* (dgp, 2016) and *Sylvia Plath in the Major Arcana* (Anchor & Plume, forthcoming 2017).

I Hope That You Are

Kept/
   awake
tonight
by the thought
of who is jumping

the barricades,

who is crossing
the borders

that you have created.

Kept
awake

by the words
they are painting
already
across
your tombstone.

Karl Vs. Richard Marx

Confusing moment
for the movement.

Affection vs. affectation,

the trickle
down
kompromat.

And I ask you what if
the painting that I have left of you

is now of cacophony,

these limbs twisted.

A machine gun filled with cartoon
hands, their thumbs in the air.

You answer that some song lyrics quoted
are just song lyrics.

Your ghost tosses
its fucking hair.

If this sounds like a diplomatic answer, it is.

If this sounds like an evasive answer,
that's because it is.

C.C. Russell lives in Wyoming with his wife and daughter. His writing has recently appeared in such places as Tahoma Literary Review, Word Riot, Rattle, and The Colorado Review. His short fiction has been nominated for a Pushcart Prize, Best Small Fictions, and Best of the Net. He has held jobs in a wide range of vocations—everything from graveyard shift convenience store clerk to retail management with stops along the way as dive bar dj and swimming pool maintenance. He has also lived in New York and Ohio. He can be found on Twitter @c_c_russell

Found poems, based on news articles and speeches by and about Donald Trump.

After the Confirmation of Betsy DeVos (From the NY Times: "Betsy DeVos Confirmed as Education Secretary, Pence Breaks Tie).

an aggressive assault. children swamped
in pages of waste. exhausted. we need
conversion therapy for wealthy. $200
million. a defection of difficulty. an
ideology of (un)freeing—money built
to dismantle. particularly weary
are low income children—she hid
her complex web of non-ethics, of
un-freedom in historic disconnect.
raise an alarm on un-filed ethics.

At the Women's March on Washington (Words from Donald Trump's Inaugural Speech)

urban sprawl of solidarity
a landscape of wind-swept
desire/demand. rusted
trapped ladies.
unstoppable
in circles we demand
our stolen tongues
unrealized depletion of
subsidized carnage—tombstones
of grandmother unrealized
and ripped we bleed
in desire.

Colleen Hamilton-Lecky is a third year Cultural Studies major at UCLA. She values poetry not only as a medium of personal expression, but also as a collective force of / for resistance. As a Teaching Artist with Get Lit—Words Ignite, her pedagogy centers around such practices of liberation, and building new languages for acceptance across the City of Los Angeles.

Jacqueline Derner Tchakalian

These Days

Repose[2]: *(repose something in) place*
something, esp. one's confidence or trust, in.

-*The New Oxford American Dictionary*

No repose in the mouth
I inhabit these days –

lies line teeth like plaque –
tongue spews colored wet

shards as though aiming
for a spittoon – spittle

obvious to all viewing Reality
TV's new show – if only

it weren't so real – incisors,
canines, molars chew meat

with grip of hurt, exclusion –
bleeding gums denote pathology

of the heart – maybe other
organs as well – the three

abnormally short frenulum
affect tongue – upper & lower

internal lips – shorten his
thoughts to 40 characters –

tighten his mouth – churn
the mix of shrinking syntax –

mean intentions to a mash
of projections – shame – bully

those he wants to control –
his handlers realize this is

his true voice – he can't change –
use his inside voice –

something some of us knew
before we were forced to

inhabit his mouth daily –
even abrupt silences are

filled with venom –
handlers learn he must

be kept on a leash – for the
sake of the neighborhoods –

fill his mouth with their
plans – until he wanders

the empty corridors of his
mind at 2 AM – discovers

a cell phone and tweets
more lies – carried around

the world – on the curve of
the world – become the news

of the day before millions
open their TV's – have their

first cup of coffee or tea –
taste of fear.

Jacqueline Derner Tchakalian, a resident of Southern California, is a poet and visual artist. Her book *The Size of Our Bed*, Red Hen Press, was published in 2015. She has appeared in St. Petersberg Review 7, Eclipse, the anthology Beyond the Lyric Moment, as well as other publications.

Rhonda Melanson

On Pennsylvania Avenue

Father Time
should have had the vasectomy

before he produced offspring
who only hatch in tandem.

Compelled to crush their shells
as atonement

eggshell pellets
feeding their heads

they lay claim to the chicken
yelling off with her head.

When PETA lines curbs
of Pennsylvania Avenue

cock of the walk tweets
it's not his fault.

Rhonda Melanson has been published in several print and online magazines, including The Boxcar Poetry Review, Quill's, Philadelphia Poets, Ascent Aspirations and the Windsor Review. In 2011, she published a chapbook called *Gracenotes* with Beret Days Press, and currently, she is featured in the Encompass IV anthology, a publication from Beret Days Press and The Ontario Poetry Society.

Beautiful Beautiful Poem

Somebody's doing the raping.
Who's doing the raping?
Who is doing the raping?
I mean, somebody's doing the raping.

I will make them stop raping.
They will pay me, oh boy will
they pay me, to make them stop raping
by building a beautiful wall.

China, Great Wall, its bank's in my building,
while Putin, who is such a strong leader,
he says, he just said this, I'm leading,
I'm such a beautiful, talented leader.

Look at these fingers, so long and beautiful
and you know what that means, I guarantee
you, no problem, only Rosie O'Donnell
and Megyn, because that's the beauty of me.

Obama, who said I'm here "still," the worst
ever president, we know wasn't born in
Hawaii, reliable sources, the first
to admit he's, believe me, no Putin.

That's why the blacks, why the Mexicans
love me, I'll totally carry their vote.
So many jobs, so many Puerto Ricans
will caddy, play baseball, you won't believe it,

so tired of all the new, fifty million,
all these great jobs, all the wins, we don't win
anymore, send the best people, Carl Icahn
loves just how great I will make us again.

These disgusting reporters, this little
Katy Turd, a 9 but still absolute scum.
I respect, really cherish Gwen Ifill,
watching NBC fail, hemorrhage loot, some

nice ones, not many, I like them, they're out
of business without me. AC360
loves just how fast I will send them back out
the beautiful door in the wall, they will pay me.

Belt it out, Freedom Kids: *Over here,*
Over there, show us your 'Meritude!
USA! It's our land! Hear us cheer!
Love this land, don't be scared to be rude . . .

Love, love, love.
It's really all you need.
Just mow the lawn and man the stove
until your fingers bleed,

then back you go to Syria, Mexico, Poland,
Anastasia, wherever. All models can stay.
Those jobs aren't seasonal, I depend
on them giving, blow *him* back to Kenya, okay?

James McManus is an American teacher, writer, and poker player. His poems have appeared in Poetry, The Atlantic, Paris Review, Irish American Poets From the Eighteenth Century to the Present, two editions of The Best American Poetry, and other magazines and anthologies. He teaches at The School of the Art Institute of Chicago.

Trumpery

Speak no trump
                we can ~~read~~ no more
we become exiled
       from what does that mean

we work sixteenhour day
we ~~speak~~ no trump
we have babies
      ~~medicine~~
we run no way
       we afraid
we hate ~~our neighbors~~
we see the raids
we hear the raids
we go no trump
       you lead us to shelter
       you ~~hold us~~ sickness
       you need our wounds
       you color ~~our thoughts~~
             and watch our bodies
       what did we study

we don't have honey
       or forests or islands
we insolent and brave
       to watch TV with murderers
       telling children to pray
       pray to the dollar
             that doesn't
we hear no trump
       only yes yes yes
       grab me more your
       obscure pillowcase
       your supply of jet fuel and plastic
       your darkened White House lawn
       growing dandelions and ragweed
we imagined differently
       your perfect factories
       expansive fairways
       skin camouflaged beaches

                    your bird babble
but we ~~speak~~ no trump
          don't know which lies
          to ~~believe~~
          let us milk the soles
          of his shoes
          and be happy   but
we no   will no   never
          be ~~happy~~

                    ~~happy~~   ~~happy~~
          on these windy days
                         gone   gone   days

Caleb Beissert is translator of *Beautiful: Translations from the Spanish* published by New Native Press in 2013. Beissert also is a poet, musician, and event organizer who frequently performs and hosts readings. Born in Washington, D.C., he now resides in Asheville, North Carolina, and serves as an editor for the online poetry journal Redheaded Stepchild.

Some Lights Go Out

Bolt-struck steers, we stood & stared
    Into those spaces in between
    Our faces & the TV screen
& waited for the floorward
        Drag of gravity on our dumb,
        Meat weight. It did not come.

Stuck-in-upright, stunned, we stayed,
    Gobs spittle-slicked & slack,
    Until that screen went black
("Have we lost power?" "I'll say—")
        & we in darkness found
        Ourselves, wound-

Woozy to the point of swoon.
    The world is a shambles. Blood
    & moan. All that here was good
Is gone. Our knocker's a buffoon.
        We've all been to the kill floor
        Swoggled by the horns.

November 8, 2016

Jay Hopler is the author of *Green Squall* and the editor (with Kimberly Johnson) of *Before the Door of God: An Anthology of Devotional Poetry*. The recipient of, among others, the Yale Series of Younger Poets Award, the Great Lakes Colleges Association New Writers Award, a fellowship from the Lannan Foundation, the Whiting Writers' Award, and the Rome Prize in Literature, his most recent book, *The Abridged History of Rainfall*, was a Finalist for the 2016 National Book Award in Poetry and was awarded the 2016 Florida Book Awards Gold Medal in Poetry.

How To Brace For Impact

For almost two decades, **I have been a professional defender.** As human beings, our capacity to damage and deceive one another still astounds me. And the ones of us with integrity, who are acutely aware of such (and have been for some time), have stood in the gap as protectors trying to dull the sharp edges of these realities from those who thought they were secure here. Or, we've taken the brunt of the blows. **I am also a Black woman.**

And now, many more of us are aware and this saddens me. Not the awareness, but because no one who's suffering wants to give their disease to the people they love so that those people can suffer, too, and at last understand. Really understand. I would have rather shielded the harshness—as if I could—and fixed it first with the help of the half-sleeping, naïve—like children. **I am a mother.** We try anyway.

And now, here we are. Many more of us can intimately answer the question, "Why are those people so angry? Why are they burning down their own neighborhoods? Why are they marching? Why don't they just get a job?"

We know it.

We know it.

We know it...

Now.

Not just in theory. We're all in. We're grown-ups. And it's uneasy.

So now we need to be sure that we are the heroes we've been waiting for. **Let's be lovers.**

Because in that, there's hope. Active hope is active love. The kind that causes us to stand for each other, together, for protection and, above all, for strategy. Because the war is made up of small battles on the ground every day. Of showing up for each other in meaningful ways. Because the answers have never been only in the hands of politicians or a chosen few, but in ours. Because it's in our pens, our unity—which doesn't mean we have to be the same in thought or action—but we have to be actively *decided* in our daily lives. Because, there is where our power has always been.

I have hope that, in this great awakening, we will at last tap into what so many writers talk about—what it means to human—then BE the humans we are called to be.

Natashia Deón is a 2017 NAACP Image Award Nominee and author of the critically-acclaimed novel, *GRACE* (Counterpoint Press), which was named a New York Times and Kirkus Review Best Book of 2016. A practicing attorney, law professor, and creator of the popular L.A.-based reading series Dirty Laundry Lit, Deón is the recipient of a PEN Center USA Emerging Voices Fellowship. Her writing has appeared in American Short Fiction, Buzzfeed, LA Review of Books, The Rumpus, Rattling Wall, and other places.

SPEAK. LOVE. FIGHT.

First 7 Days (in microverse)

The ink is
a conduit for
resistance

Fuck a grant,
now artists must go
ski mask route

Pulled a pen
and stabbed them in their
conscience

White people,
go argue "race" with
white people

Keep selling
mythologies like
"God-given"

They fear the
inhumanity
they give us

Don't salute
flag some of them will
hang you with

Oligarch,
oil company
with army

The rule is
Laws are given,
rights, taken

Frump made it
so that Biff can leave
sheets at home

Stop trying
to make molehills from
swastikas

We should knock
the genocide out
of them all

Find the place
the enemy breathes
and crush it

Melanin
means no eclipse for
Sun Children

Billy Tuggle is a South Side Chicago native, recording artist, slam champion, mentor, HipHop culturalist and parent. He has authored several chapbooks and two collections of poetry, *Conscience Under Pressure* and *The Way of the B-Boy*. Billy is an organizer for long-running Chicago open mic In One Ear, and for the Mental Graffiti poetry slam. He tours regularly, performing and facilitating workshops across North America.

BillyTuggle.net || Facebook.com/backpackfiles

What Is the #Resistance? It's a SPIN

The poster board and postcard markets are hot again. Not since the Vietnam War—half a century ago—have so many made so many signs. Our local post office ran out of postcards.

In record time, millions of feet have taken to the streets and met up in coffee shops, living rooms houses of worship, and town halls to write postcards, press keys, and pigeonhole representatives in support of the (hashtagged) #resistance.

The earliest massive indicator of the #resistance came about in barely ten weeks from its original proposal. With no single overarching organization or leader, nearly four and possibly as many as six million people turned out in 914 cities around the world on January 21, 2017.

A week later, rallies erupted on a few hours' notice in airports, cities, and small towns around the country—from LAX ("throngs") to Pittsfield, Mass. (1500) to Rutland, VT (300, eyewitness account).

More than 7000 Indivisible groups have gelled along with likely at least as many Women's March Huddles, as well as hundreds of what my seven-year-old grandson calls "the rights" rallies. And then there are the "welcome home" town halls with Congressional representatives. And prep for the upcoming marches (Trump Taxes March, March for Science, The Immigrants March, the National Pride March—and that just gets us to June). What is going on? How did all this happen?

One thing is clear. We're not being paid. In fact, it's costing us to show up, foregoing work, traveling, buying stamps. And we're not wasting time deliberating about whether to participate.

The original case in point? The Women's March. Right after the election, the Washington Post reported, Teresa Shook, a retired Hawaiian attorney in despair over the result, asked friends how to put up a Facebook events page to announce her intent to march in the capital. Within a day, 10,000 others agreed to march too.

Likewise with the original immigration order—only faster. People flooded airports within hours. Then came back again. Lawyers offering free services set up shop on concourse floors.

Why is this continuing? What is bringing people into the streets again and again, requiring that they add a line item for protest in their mental budgets? How *does* word spread so quickly to so many places without a single leader or organization or news channel barking orders?

Speedy, pervasive social media provides the technology explanation, of course, i.e. post on Facebook and sit back while the Likes, Comments, and Shares pour in. But it doesn't account for the sociology that is propelling millions into action in no time.

For a still-germane answer, consider the work of anthropologists Luther Gerlach and Virginia Hine, who published their landmark book, *People, Power, Change*, in 1970. Studying two radically different social movements—the Black Power movement and the Pentecostals, they found them to be virtually identical regardless of their diametrically opposed ideologies. They had the same styles of leadership, the same organizational structures, and the same adherence to core beliefs.

Hine later encapsulated their findings in an article with a hard-to-remember title, "The Basic Paradigm of a Future Socio-Cultural System," which, she predicted, would become the prevailing organizational mode for the years to come. "Wherever people organize themselves to change some aspect of society," she wrote, "a non-bureaucratic but very effective form of organizational structure seems to emerge." She called them SPINs—Segmented Polycephalous Ideological Networks. Non-intuitive, perhaps, but bear with.

Each part, each constituent organization stands on its own and is self-sufficient, in her terms, *segmented*.

Many leaders, not one, steer these groups, a concept taken from the structure of some African tribes. *Polycephalous* literally means many (poly) heads (cephalous).

Members share abiding values and beliefs—*ideologies*—that bind them together in opposition to the established order.

And finally, in employing (and presaging) perhaps the most overused word of the internet age, she named the decentralized, horizontally linked organizations that tie people across boundaries, *networks*.

The many groups of the #resistance—both pre-existing and newborn—are independent of one another, "segmented." There is no #Resistance HQ—and if any organization were to claim that title, it would likely be quickly delegitimized.

The "ideology" that binds the #resistance is many-faceted, appearing more or less precise depending on the prevailing issue: to respond to the administration's assaults on [fill in the blank— African-Americans, Mexicans, women, Muslims, refugees, justices, Jews, the press...the list goes on].

The "leaders" of the participating groups are both ad hoc and official, either way numerous, as per Hine. There is no "head" of the #resistance. Few, I'd wager, could name Teresa Shook or the three women who became heads (note plural) of the Women's March.

The #resistance is certainly a "network" not a hierarchy. No "I alone can fix it" autocrat issues edicts. With the not-so-faint echo of "Stronger Together" and new rallying cries like "She Persisted" drawing more people into the fray, the #resistance is most definitely a SPIN, in this case, a network of networks.

Jessica Lipnack, author of six books, including *The Age of the Network*, is co-chair of the Buckminster Fuller Institute and is writing a novel about the return of Fuller's great-aunt, the 19th-century feminist writer Margaret Fuller. She lives in Cornwall, VT.

On the Anniversary of Kristallnacht, Donald Trump is Elected President

It starts with breaking glass,
a brick thrown,
Jewish storefront shattered.
Businesses destroyed.
The vile Other punished.
(All that has been worked for
in ruins.)

If I didn't know,
the German word sounds pretty,
tinkles, conjures flutes of champagne
raised in toast.

If we didn't know.

Numb, stunned, tearful,
some of us get passports, put
our houses up for sale.
Others start the work.

We try to soothe the children, promise
to protect the weak. "If he makes
Muslims register,
we'll say we're Muslim."

Still, the nuclear codes.
The blighted planet.
Klan members dancing on a bridge.
The way fracked water burns.

First reports: Hijabs ripped off,
a gay man stabbed.

Protests begin.
Our hearts are breaking.
How the pieces catch the light.

"Trump has Won the Presidency"

I will find beauty.
I will hunt for it
and force myself to see.
These lilies, for example, crowded
in a slender vase, still fresh
from my daughter's combination
bat mitzvah/quinceanera.
I will not see them as vulvas
ready to grab.
I will not focus on
how all of them are white.
If not these flowers, trees.
Or grass, sky, mountains,
sidewalks bright with children's chalk.
Surely something can force my eyes
from images of swastikas
and "Die Nigger" on buildings,
can make our broken country turn the other way.
There must be beauty fierce enough to save us.

Alison Stone is the author of five poetry collections, including *Ordinary Magic,* (NYQ Books, 2016), *Dangerous Enough* (Presa Press 2014), and *They Sing at Midnight,* which won the 2003 Many Mountains Moving Poetry Award and was published by Many Mountains Moving Press. Her poems have appeared in The Paris Review, Poetry, Ploughshares, Barrow Street, Poet Lore, and a variety of other journals and anthologies. She has been awarded Poetry's Frederick Bock Prize and New York Quarterly's Madeline Sadin award. She is also a painter and the creator of The Stone Tarot. A licensed psychotherapist, she has private practices in NYC and Nyack. She is currently editing an anthology of poems on the Persephone/Demeter myth.

Nina Mariah Donovan

Nasty Woman
-As read at the Woman's March by Ashley Judd

I'm a Nasty Woman.
Not as nasty as a man who looks like he bathes in Cheeto dust.
Not as nasty a man who is a diss track to America.
From Back to broken Back he's stomped on, his words are just more white
noise ruining this national anthem.
I'm not as nasty as confederate flags being tattooed across my city;
maybe the South actually is going to rise again.
Or maybe it never really fell
because we're still drowning in vanilla coated power.
Slavery has just been reinterpreted into the prison system.
Black lives are still in shackles and graves just for being black in front of
people who see melanin as animal skin.
Tell me of a decade that didn't have traces of white hoods burning up our
faith in humanity.
I'm not as nasty as a swastika painted on a pride flag
and I didn't know that devils could be resurrected but I feel Hitler
in these streets
a mustache traded in for a Toupee
the Nazis renamed The Cabinet
conversion therapy the new gas chamber,
shaming and electrocuting the gay out of America
turning rainbows into suicide notes.
I'm not as nasty as racism, or fraud, or homophobia, sexual assault,
transphobia, white supremacy, white privilege, ignorance, or misogyny.
Not as nasty as trading girls like Pokemon before their bodies
have even evolved.
Not as nasty as your own daughter being your favorite sex symbol
like wet dreams infused with your own genes.
But yeah!
I'm a nasty woman.
A phunky
Crusty
Bitchy
Loud
Nasty woman.
Not as nasty as the combo of Trump and Pence being served into my
voting booth,
but I'm nasty like the battles women fought to get me in that voting booth.
Nasty like the fight to close the wage gap.

Nasty like conversations trying to remind people there is such thing as a wage gap.

Tell me that this is only because women usually go into lower paying fields.

So why did last year's top actresses make less than half of what the top actors did?

Do you realize that the World Cup shelf of the U.S. men's soccer team is as empty as Trump's promises

But the women's team has scored three World Cups,

In 2015, brought in 20 million more dollars in revenue than the men's team, but is still paid 75% less?

See even when women go into high paying careers, their wages are still cut with blades sharpened by testosterone.

Tell me why the work of a black woman and a Hispanic women is only worth 63 and 54 percent of a white man's privileged paycheck?

This is not a feminist myth;

this is inequality.

So we are not here to be debunked

We are here to be respected.

We are here to be nasty

like blood stained bedsheets.

In case you forgot,

women don't choose when or if they get their periods!

Trust me, if we could we would!

We don't like throwing away our favorite pairs of underwear!

But men can choose to not have sex

and they know how to live without a full head of hair,

so why are tampons and pads still taxed, but Viagra and Rogaine isn't?

Is your erection really more important than protecting the messy parts of my womanhood?

Is the thinning of your hair really more embarrassing than the period-staining of my jeans?

I know it seems petty to complain about a few extra cents

but it's just the finishing touch on a pile of change I have yet to feel in this country.

So don't try to justify our injustices with excuses that smell like your security when you're walking alone to the bathroom

or your car

or down the street.

Security my eyes have yet to see

They're too busy praying to my feet

so you don't mistake eye contact for wanting physical contact

I've been zipping up my smile so you don't think I want to unzip your jeans.

I know you forget to examine the reflection of your own privilege.

You may be afraid of the truth

but I'm not afraid to be honest,

I'm not afraid to be nasty.
Yeah I'm nasty
like the struggle of women still beating equality into the world,
because our rights have been beaten out of us for too long.
And our fight will continue to embody our nastiness.
I'm nasty like red, white, and blue bruises.
Nasty like Elizabeth, Amelia, Rosa, Eleanor, Condoleezza, Sonia, Malala, Michelle.
Our mothers, our sisters, us sisters are all nasty like history
and our pussies
ain't for grabbing.
They're for reminding you that our walls are stronger than America's ever will be.
They're for birthing new generations of
Filthy
Vulgar
Bossy
Brave
Proud
Nasty women.
So if you a nasty woman
say hell yeah.

Nina Mariah Donovan is a 19 year old spoken word artist in the greater Nashville area. She is a Sociology major at Middle Tennessee State University, and hopes to one day become either a Women and Gender Studies, or Social Problems professor. She currently has an EP out titled *What A Time To Be Nasty*, which can be found on Spotify, iTunes, Tidal, Amazon Music, Apple Music, etc. You can connect with her on Instagram (itsninamariah), Facebook (Nina Mariah Donovan), SoundCloud (ninamariahpoetry) and Twitter (ninathehyena_)!

Liberal Minded

Liberal minded
You've been blinded
Lookin' for true democracy
You can't find it

We're stuck in this shit
Bureaucratically binded
The system is broke
And that's the way they designed it

You're feelin' a li'l strange
This ain't the change that you hoped for
Startin' to wonder if it matters
Who you fuckin' vote for

Capitalism can't exist
Without a class war
So gimme a job
Or gimme the money outta the cash drawer

You think your efforts
Make a difference
When politics are corrupted
By corporate interests

And things won't change
One damn bit
If you keep on suckin'
On Uncle Sam's dick

It remains constant
When Congress is always in conflict
And corrupt Governors
Become convicts

We gotsta get the people
Together
We been try'na do some good
But we gotsta do better

Kao Ra Zen, lifelong poet, painter, and performer, hails from Chicago, IL. His writings cover a range of topics, be it personal narrative, stream of consciousness, or spiritual in nature. Kao works professionally as a tour boat captain on the Chicago waterways. He has served as a Science Mentor in CPS grade schools, hosted free creativity workshops, and traveled to El Salvador as a volunteer to assist in the installation of solar panels. A multi talented artist who has exhibited and performed throughout Chicago and in Germany, Kao Ra Zen is busy recording for his debut solo album, *A Melancholy King*.

Juliane Tran

Youth

When this blight of narrow-
mindedness is over,
we'll know how long we knelt in naiveté
to wait for the powerful to make amends.

The barred cradle or prison, the doctor or lawman's
counter, the places where our pain had to flow like
cold water, were also the meccas where we learned
that living is a purposeful
breaking, and entering.

Juliane Tran is an aspiring polyglot.

I lie in the road remembering

my friend who took out a Glock
and shot towards the bus unexpectedly
I still love him
let me hear you say:
I love him

He is 63rd street,
a little boy heart-starved
for America, cruelty spraying
in its pot.
Who is unknown to cruelty?
Even you in your perfect body
a hidden monster hungry,
you ate no better.
Pushing your tongue
into a promise
in the dark
is easy.
I remember running
leaps of nerve
an attack plane
let me tell you
my eyes welling
with a spirit or rifle
brimming over
what they shout at me
Don't get too smart
as I sharpen instead
of sing

This is not hell you are swimming in baby

it's my womb this is our side street
you got a hold of my demons
in there a surge of lilac in something already
dying baby you are the skull of your mother
holding on fast and guess what you might live
yet you might be in one piece or be free too much
alone in your pain you still fly like a boat
be the resistance   be the resistance
you're so beautiful you break my eyes once you were a feather
now you crash in on America breathing heavy into a sheer blouse
I pray your heart stays in one piece
my heart is hurling stones at whatever hunts you
we move to each other
steps constantly blooming.

Annmarie O'Connell is a lifelong resident of the South side of Chicago. Her work has appeared or is forthcoming in Sixth Finch, Juked, Verse Daily, Slipstream, SOFTBLOW, Vinyl Poetry, Curbside Splendor, Escape Into Life, 2River View and many other wonderful journals. Her second chapbook, *Eleanor*, came out last year with dancing girl press. Her first full-length collection of poems, *Your Immaculate Heart*, was released with Trio House Press in 2016. Her third chapbook, *hello*, was released this summer with Yellow Flag Press. She can also be found here: annmarieoconnell.com.

To the Man

To the man who doesn't know my name,
I know your name,
And I wish I didn't,
I know you won't read this,
But I'm writing this letter anyway.
To the man who doesn't know my name,
I almost died last year.
I am part of the 99.5%.
ACA saved my life.
I know that doesn't matter to you,
But I'm writing it down anyway.
When you are putting on your makeup,
And rehearsing for your latest gig,
People like me,
Are dying.
I hope you enjoy yourself,
When you're playing puppet master to all your politician friends.
I know you don't care about this,
But I do.
When you're in the White House,
I hope you enjoy looking down on people like me.
I live in a subsidized apartment,
Where,
No lie,
Two people got shot
Last month.
I hope you enjoy yourself,
When you're moving people
Like chess pieces
In pursuit of power.
I know you won't read this letter,
But I need to write this.
You are not my president.
You are the President of Skeletons.
I know you don't know my name,
But I wish you did.

Elizabeth Stansberry is a secretary at Prosper Portland. She also works as security on call for the Portland Art Museum. Miss Stansberry has been a poet for 3 decades now. At age 8, she started writing poems and stories for her friends at school. In 2002, she graduated from Idaho State University with a BA in English. She has written several manuscripts and hopes to publish them soon. In 2009, she published *The waiting room* in the poetry journal, The Eclectic Muse. In 2012, she published her poem, *The first step*, in Oregon Artswatch. She has also had poems published in several anthologies. Miss Stansberry volunteers as a poetry teacher at the EMO Day Center. She currently lives in Portland, Oregon.

After the elections went to shit

my NARAL sticker came
two weeks to inauguration

Nasty Women Vote
stock patriotic backdrop

I'm not a crier but
I tear up holding it

crumble the envelope
into my recycling bin

my friends write op-eds
plan marches

I get drawn in
to Facebook fights

read poetry research
try to write

maybe if I made
that extra 33%

I could afford to fly
to Washington

instead I sign petitions
join local groups

listen to my students
my kids who only remember

Obama's America
women as contenders

my bumper sticker stays
on the kitchen counter

reminds me to take responsibility
every time I eat

Keri Withington is passionate about studying social issues and advocating for social equity. Professionally, she is an educator and author based in the shadow of the Smoky Mountains. Her work has previously appeared in numerous journals and anthologies, recently including Blue Fifth Review, Feminine Inq., and Calamus Journal.

It Begins with No

This is a time for resistance. That's what I hear these days. (Fact: it always was.)

So what does this resistance look like? Specifically, as a writer and publisher, what does it look like to me?

Resistance always begins with NO. No to tyrants. No to registries. No to surrender. We march. We protest. We sit in. We scream. We study and vote and argue and gather and battle.

Specifically for me, as a writer and as a small publisher, I have to say no in this world in which I work and live.

It's not enough to just make art. That time has passed. We have to force accountability in whatever world we live in daily, which for me is the publishing world. We are disgusted when Simon & Schuster imprints shell out six figures for Milo Yiannopoulos's hate speech (except those who mistakenly think this is freedom of speech issue).

But so much of that goes on daily unnoticed in the indie lit world, in the poetry world, and even in the resistance itself. A Writers Resist event includes a person who has compared literary activists to ISIS. An editor brings some of the best writers in the country together…and sets up a reading at a place famous for stealing public money and for being sued for racist practices.

Just because you write poems or books, it doesn't mean you're resisting. Just because you own a bookstore, it doesn't mean you aren't the source of exclusion and erasure. And running a publishing company doesn't absolve you from predatory and discriminatory behavior.

No is a difficult and complicated word. But resistance begins with no. And like everything that begins, it begins in the places where we live and work.

Chiwan Choi is the author of 3 collections of poetry, *The Flood* (Tía Chucha Press, 2010), *Abductions* (Writ Large Press, 2012), and *The Yellow House* (CCM, 2017). He wrote, presented, and destroyed the novel *Ghostmaker* throughout the course of 2015. Chiwan is a partner at Writ Large Press, a downtown Los Angeles based indie publisher, focused on using literary arts to resist, disrupt, and transgress.

Amanda Palmer

FUCK THAT!

A protest song in three verses.

Written on the day of and performed at the Sydney women's march,
January 21st, 2017.

[*Enter* AMANDA *and* UKULELE.]

AMANDA. frank sinatra's mother had a funny little nickname
they called her "hatpin dolly"
and i wonder what you're thinking
the origin's disturbing
(and i'm sorry for the trigger)
she earned it from the back-alley abortions she'd deliver...

but that was many years ago
and THANK GOD all that's changed
the right to vote
the right to choose
the right to keep our names

but now a new regime is gearing up for the attack...
i don't know 'bout you
but i'm not keen on
dolly's
nickname
coming
back

[AMANDA *wields her* UKULELE *aloft*]

AMANDA. when i say FUCK, you say THAT!
FUCK!
CROWD. THAT!
AMANDA. FUCK!
CROWD. THAT!

AMANDA. when i say NEVER, you say BACK!!

NEVER!!
 CROWD. BACK!!
 AMANDA. NEVER!!
 CROWD. BACK!!
 AMANDA. i used to think that progress was a single forward line...
it's 2017, folks: WHAT THE FUCK IS GOING ON??!?!?!!

[much cheering and hooting and hollering - the sound of tambourines rattling angrily]

 AMANDA. *[spoken]* I JUST HEARD THAT THERE WERE BETWEEN
FIVE AND TEN THOUSAND PEOPLE AT THIS MARCH

[crowd goes wild]

AND THAT THIS IS THE BIGGEST MARCH FOR WOMEN'S
RIGHTS IN SYDNEY IN A GENERATION!!

[crowd goes even wilder]

 AMANDA. back in 1800 the mere thought of it seemed wild
that all of us were equal – every woman man and child –
this was back when you'd get lynched due to the color of your skin
and a woman's worth was measured by the marriage she was in
but that was years ago before we flattened sex and race
(well, except for all these muslims who they'd like to just erase)
how 'bout we build a wall around them all and make them pay?
if martin luther king was here i wonder what he'd say...?

[spoken] i think he'd say:

when i say FUCK, you say THAT!
FUCK!
 CROWD. THAT!
 AMANDA. FUCK!
 CROWD. THAT!
 AMANDA. when i say NEVER, you say BACK!!
NEVER!!
 CROWD. BACK!!
 AMANDA. NEVER!!
 CROWD. BACK!!

 AMANDA. it can't be happening – can it? – that these xenophobes will win
their battle for supremacy... IT'S 2017!!!!

*[*AMANDA's *microphone begins to droop, apparently losing its erection. laughter from*

crowd. AMANDA *makes some off-color microphone/viagra jokes and stalls for time...*]

AMANDA. [*spoken*] LET'S JUST DO SOME "FUCK THATS" FOR PRACTICE!!
EVERYBODY READY?

FUCK!
CROWD. THAT!

AMANDA. FUCK!
CROWD. THAT!

AMANDA. FUCK!
CROWD. THAT!

AMANDA. FUCK!
CROWD. THAT!
AMANDA. FUCK!
CROWD. THAT!
AMANDA. FUCK!
CROWD. THAT!

AMANDA. FUCK!
CROWD. THAT!
AMANDA. FUCK!
CROWD. THAT!
AMANDA. [*spoken*] YOU GUYS ARE REALLY GOOD AT THIS!

[*cheers*]

AMANDA. america's been struggling forever with her history
slavery
misogyny
land stolen in the first place
[AMANDA *spoken sarcastically aside to the australians*] you guys don't know
anything about that, do you?

[*laughter*]

but with the bad stuff came the good
and with it some amendments...
the civil rights
the marriage rights
the vulnerable protected
i have a little boy now and it's hard not to feel horror

i can't let him see i'm frightened by the shape of his tomorrow
this might be insurmountable
and the horror here to stay...
we could just give up on fighting, everyone,
WHADDAYA SAY?

[AMANDA, *strumming her* UKULELE *with extreme enthusiasm*]

when i say FUCK, you say THAT!
FUCK!
   CROWD. THAT!
   AMANDA. FUCK!
   CROWD. THAT!
   AMANDA. when i say NEVER, you say STOP!!
NEVER!!
   CROWD. STOP!!
   AMANDA. NEVER!!
   CROWD. STOP!!
   AMANDA. never stop sharing your stories, my friends!!
never stop fighting this fucked president!!

[*THE CROWD ERUPTS WITH A PROFOUND COMBINATION OF
ANGER AND JOY*]

I'LL SEE YOU HERE IN 2021!!!!
                                    [*Exeunt.*]

Amanda Palmer is a fearless singer, songwriter, playwright, blogger and an audaciously expressive pianist who simultaneously embraces, and explodes, traditional frameworks of music, theater and art.

Amanda first came to prominence as one half of the internationally acclaimed punk cabaret duo The Dresden Dolls. In May of 2012 she made international news pre-selling her new album, *Theatre is Evil*, along with related merchandise and experiences via Kickstarter. *Theatre is Evil* went on to debut in the Billboard Top 10 when it was released on Sept. 11, 2012, and has been released in over 20 countries on her own label, 8ft records.

Amanda was invited to present a TED Talk at TED's 2013 Conference. To date her Talk, The Art of Asking, has been viewed more than 7.7 million times worldwide. 2013 also saw the release of *An Evening with Neil Gaiman & Amanda Palmer*—a 3 CD collection of tracks culled from a live tour with her husband and best-selling author Neil Gaiman.

2014 found Amanda expanding her philosophy into a book after the success of her TED Talk. *The Art of Asking* was released world-wide on Nov. 11th and made the New York Time's Best Seller List. She is now making songs and art with the financial backing of over 10,500 committed patrons on the new crowdfunding/subscription website Patreon.Com.

With 2015 given over to the creation of Amanda and Neil's son Anthony, 2016 saw Amanda back into creating art for her Patrons and visiting Australia for a three month solo tour over their Summer. 2017 saw release of her collaboration with Legendary Pink Dots founder Edward Ka-Spel *I Can Spin a Rainbow*, with an accompanying tour of the US and Europe.

Amanda
David Mack

I WILL NOT BOW DOWN Donald Trump

I Will Not Bow Down
to your Reign of Fear Based Racist Street Bully Tyranny
I Will Not Bow Down Donald Trump
I Will Not Bow Down
to your Racially Purified White America
to your Dividing and Conquering the USA
I will not Bow Down Donald Trump
I Will Not Bow Down
to your Racist Fear Based Power Mongering
in the name of Democracy!!!
Donald Trump
I pledge allegiance
to those who were here before you
to those who will be here after you are gone
Donald Trump
I pledge allegiance
to the woman I love
I pledge allegiance to my children my grandchildren my godchildren
and all my children to come
I pledge allegiance
to my friends and allies
my guides and angels
both seen and unseen
Donald Trump
I pledge allegiance
to poetry to music to art
to the literary renaissance
to the global literary community
I pledge allegiance to the Beat to the Outsider
I pledge allegiance to meditation to stillness
to magic to beautiful mysticism to ecstasy
to AH and AHA
to the Big Bang Epiphany
to altered states of consciousness
I pledge allegiance
to seeing

into the occult the unknown
to seeing
into every day into the ordinary
and being amazed
I pledge allegiance to the Sacred and the Profane
to gnostical turpitude
I pledge allegiance to my physical body
and to the knowledge that I am more than
my physical body
I pledge allegiance to seeing more than
the physical world and to those
of higher frequency vibration
and consciousness
I pledge allegiance to passing through
the Sacred Fire
to entering the upper chamber of the
golden pyramid
to levitating over the open sarcophagus
to out of body experience
I pledge allegiance to the hottest sex
and to gentle affection
I pledge allegiance to fractal geometry
the geometry of clouds and coastlines
to 2×2 equaling 5
I pledge allegiance to Failure
to failing as no other dare fail
I pledge allegiance to taking risks
to holy daring
to nam myoho renge kyo
to accepting responsibility for my own actions
I pledge allegiance to not achieving
the Donald Trump Dream of Success
Donald Trump
I pledge allegiance to trees to green grass
to brown earth to wildflowers of every color
to wilderness to turquoise skies
to rivers lakes and seas
to healing the earth
Donald Trump
I pledge allegiance to the Creative Forces of the universe
to the Word and to Silence

I pledge allegiance to Dreams
I pledge allegiance to Birth to the Journey and to Death
I pledge allegiance
to Candor to Sincerity to Laughter and to Irony
I pledge allegiance to Passion to Compassion
to Empathy and to helping those in need
Donald Trump
I pledge allegiance to Resurrection of the Heart
Donald Trump
I pledge allegiance to NOT hurting anyone
NO
Donald Trump
I WILL NOT BOW DOWN

Poet, writer, editor, publisher, scholar, professor, activist Ron Whitehead grew up on a farm in Kentucky. He attended The University of Louisville and Oxford University. As poet and writer he is the recipient of numerous state, national, and international awards and prizes including The All Kentucky Poetry Prize, The Yeats Club of Oxford's Prize for Poetry, and many others. In 2006 Dr. John Rocco (NYC) nominated Ron for The Nobel Prize in Literature. He was recently inducted into his high school's (Ohio County High) Hall of Fame, representing his 1968 graduating class.

Ron has edited and published the works of such luminaries as His Holiness The Dalai Lama, President Jimmy Carter, Hunter S. Thompson, Thomas Merton, Jack Kerouac, John Updike, Wendell Berry, Andy Warhol, Yoko Ono, BONO, Allen Ginsberg, Hunter S. Thompson, William S. Burroughs, Rita Dove, Douglas Brinkley, Robert Hunter, Amiri Baraka, Lawrence Ferlinghetti, and hundreds more.

Ron has produced over 2,000 Arts Events, Happenings, and Festivals throughout Europe and the USA. He has performed thousands of shows around the world with some of the best musicians and bands on the planet. He recently returned from a Scandinavia Tour with French rock band Blaak Heat and from New York City where his new book *blistered asphalt on dixie highway: Kentucky Basketball is Poetry in Motion* was released at the historic Poets House.

Ron's work has been translated into nearly 20 languages. He is the author of 30 books and 40 cds. His newest book is, *Quest for Self in the Ocean of Consciousness: Ibsen, Hamsun, Munch, Joyce: The Origins of Modernism and Expressionism.*

Ron Whitehead's official website is tappingmyownphone.com

Down is the New Up

I have not written about the last (general) election. At first I did not want to add to the noise out there (and there is a lot of NOISE out there!) then I didn't want to go off half cocked then I wasn't sure which direction to fire because bullets ricochet in funny directions when you live in a bubble that is floating like the ghosts of Joe Hill, Eugene Debbs and Caesar Chavez and this got me to thinking... If a ghost can walk through walls, why doesn't he fall through the floor?

At that point I realized I was on the edge of something really big, standing upon a great precipice. And that is probably not a good time to put your best foot forward. I mean, I like the metaphor of hell being beneath us 'cause sometimes ya gotta go through hell. Sometimes, ya gotta get down there and wrestle 'dem demons. Hell, sometimes ya gotta get down there and jello wrestle 'dem demons. Just remember, when ya go through hell, ya gotta keep going. You'll come out on the other side wondering why everyone is speaking in an Australian accent.

"America First" and "Make America Great Again" are contradictory statements. America will be great again, when she sees herself IN the world, not AS the world. America will be great again when she treats her neighbors like she would herself. She will be great again when she realizes that "first" implies there is a race in the first place, an order to the universe, in which one could be, or become, "First."

Not America First, Earth First.

America will be great again when she takes a global view that does not seek to take advantage of the rest of the world: labor standards in Bangladesh, environmental laws in Mexico, when she ends offshore bank accounts. America will be great again when she begins to lift up the rest of the world, export our job safety standards, export our living wage concepts, export our Unions, export our solidarity, not so America will be first, so that the people of the world are first.

In a world where Down is the New Up, what he is proposing is Nationalism, pure and simple. And the infrastructure spending, the wall building that is being proposed is well, socialism. It is (in fact) National Socialism.

Yes... that is Nazi.

So if WE are looking for a way forward let us grab every crowbar, every monkey wrench, every guitar, every paintbrush and use them as a tool to pry the socialism away from National Socialism and smother the nationalism with a new global perspective.

America will be great when she sheds her concept of Corporate Oligarchy.

WHEN IT COMES TO SOCIAL ISSUES:

This Cabinet of Billionaires couldn't really care less about any of this whako conservative agenda. Oh sure, they will give money to the church to show they "care" about social issues, but we all know giving money to the church doesn't make you a good person any more than buying tickets to the game makes you a third–baseman. What the church offers to the rich is—people. The only thing in the world the 1% does not have is people, 99% of us to be exact.

But wait a second… within the 99% a whole lotta working class folks voted for Trump! Poor people. MY people! What did we do SO wrong that makes your average redneck think a guy descending from the Heavens on a gold plated escalator in a Manhattan skyscraper has their interests at heart? Why did they work so hard building a scaffold from which they can hang a noose and then fight each other over who gets to hang themselves first? Is that the America First he is talking about?

NO!

To make the world GREAT again, WE have to burst our own bubbles! We have to go out there and yes, befriend a redneck. DO NOT INSULT THEM! Befriend them (us). If each and every one of us goes out and befriends, and turns around one Trump Supporter we could make America Great again, and THAT America maybe (just maybe) COULD make the world great again. Get the red necks on our side. Make them lose their base, because in short, as long as there is something resembling a government, the rich need large numbers of people to support them, so they will say or do anything to stay in office.

(Hear this!)

They don't actually care about these social issues.
They don't NEED to care.
They don't LIVE in society.
They have their own police force.
They have their own schools, their own hospitals.
Soon they will have their own military.

I am not afraid of Iran getting the bomb.
I am afraid of Exxon getting the bomb.

Walk softly and carry a big carrot, because like I've always said, if you think there is a cutting edge than you ain't on it. Which is why I don't think this is that "edgy" of a thought—if the rich can cross the lines between right and wrong like ghosts walk through walls, maybe it is time they also fell through the floor. Maybe they will go straight to hell, and maybe (just maybe), we will all come out on the other side.

Poet and storyteller Chris Chandler is as hilarious and entertaining as he is provocative and rabble-rousing, delivering vignettes about politics and modern culture with the fire of a Baptist Preacher. His appearances are insightful tales of a world gone slightly mad, accompanied by a wide variety of musical styles. He has performed on thousands of stages across North America, working with such legendary figures as Allen Ginsberg, Pete Seeger, Mojo Nixon and Ani DiFranco. The late great Utah Phillips called Chris "the best performance poet I have ever seen."

Another Outlaw Manifesto

When wood's damp,
a spark's sometimes not
enough to get a fire going.
So, we spend some days
a bit colder than others.

But when you are born
for this lean life out here
on the knife-edge of art,
you huddle close to other
outlaws, find your hidden
caves, and stick the shit out.

      A good, stiff scotch
      doesn't hurt either.

So what if the well-polished
ass of ignorance is yanking
the chains and reins of this
worn-thin but decent country?

That's no reason to leave it.
Just stick to your paint-
and ink-loaded guns.

Because thinkers—
when they realize
they've stopped thinking
for a while—start thinking
again, and eventually out-think
the non-thinkers who slipped
through the cracks in
the floorboards of hell.

It's a tired old plot for
books and the big stage:

      a league of buffoons, limp
      dicks, and poodle-fakers
      running a kakistocracy.

And we have no time now
for profound surprise, or
righteous indignation.

We all need
to get back
to tending
the fire.

Nathan Brown is an author, singer–songwriter, photographer, and award-winning poet who recently served as the Poet Laureate of Oklahoma for 2013 and 2014. Though he lives now in Wimberley, Texas with his wife, Ashley, he has always considered Oklahoma his home.

Nathan taught at the University of Oklahoma for many years, but now travels widely, offering readings, house concerts, creativity workshops, and musical performances in an effort to bring back the hint of a smile and the hope for a good story in poems… poems unafraid of making sense… poems that carry us to better places.

Nathan is an accomplished poet and songwriter who has performed from the Walt Whitman Birthplace Association in Long Island, NY to the Sisters Folk Festival in Oregon, as well as the Woody Guthrie Festival in Okemah, Oklahoma, to name a few. His performances of poetry have been likened to musical concerts, and, in fact, he now makes a big part of his living from house concerts and live shows that combine songs and poems.

He's published fourteen books and also worked as a professional songwriter and musician for decades in and around Oklahoma City, Nashville, and Austin. He has performed in venues such as the Bluebird in Nashville, the Cactus Cafe in Austin, the Mucky Duck in Houston, and the Blue Door in Oklahoma City, as well as overseas in Israel and Russia. His most recent album, *Gypsy Moon*, was recorded at Blue Rock Studios just outside of Austin.

He holds an interdisciplinary Ph.D. in Creative and Professional Writing from the University of Oklahoma. And he currently teaches History of the Arts and Humanities courses for the Liberal Studies Department at the University of Oklahoma, as well as Introduction to Songwriting for Austin Community College, and he served as the Artist in Residence at the University of Central Oklahoma.

What to do while awaiting the Angel of Death, or, the Angel of Life

Plant softly. Majestically. And always,
con *respeto*. Y *amor.* Seeds are our children
from a different mother. Nights are our
Angels, restoring pools of rest and planning
Even in times when we hide, secret blood painted
on our doors with brushes only we can see, with
plumas only we still remember how to use, even then
the Angels still remember how to find us, huddled,
shivering, praying, breathing in our dreams for dawn,
sueños del amanecer, sueños de la libertad,
squeezing all the seeds we can, in each palm
awaiting just one drop of stubborn sunlight
one ungestapoed heartfull of dirt
one action brave enough
to grow
    resistance
    change
    love

Dedicated to my mother who was born the year women got the vote; who requested a ballot by mail in August, 2016 so she could vote for Hillary in October; who made her 99th birthday in December and then died in January, so as to pre-empt the Inauguration of D. Trump with her funeral.

Dr. Carmen Tafolla, a Mexican-American whose family has lived in San Antonio since the 1700s, is the author of more than 20 books, and the winner of numerous national and international awards, including recognition for "work which gives voice to the peoples and cultures of this land." The 2015 State Poet Laureate of Texas, she is a Professor of Transformative Children's Literature at UT San Antonio, and is at work on the biography of 1930s Civil Rights Leader Emma Tenayuca. She has appeared in several videos, including HBO Habla Texas, where she explains how "We didn't cross the border; the border crossed us."

Emily Rose

Denial for Lent

I'm not gonna write about war today. I don't want
to talk about bodies dragged, a child in the sand
blood trickling from her ear. I won't talk about
the ships in genital metaphor or call a bomb
Mother today. If I don't talk about it, maybe
it will go away. Like my hacking cough
or the three months since I've talked to my father.
I don't want to be clever or loud or angry or any
version of indignation in repose. It's hot and
I'm selfish when I am sweating. Marches
make me anxious and I can't stand making phone calls
even to my father. I'm not making signs. I'm not
pretending like reposting means I really care
today. I weep and drink and smoke more
when things are awful. I've purchased 6 dresses
in 3 days and made as many donations to offset
the inaction. I pay other people to fight and don't
write about how many people have died this week.
I can't keep count. The number makes me weep
and drink and smoke more. I coo at babies. I focus
on their easy joy. I pour waters for people and make
jokes and try to help the awkward first dates move
the courtship along. They don't want to talk about
North Korea, David Dao, MOABs, marching vigils
for the hundreds of dead Chicago children or how
long it took to say all their names, the list of missing
black girls, the list of dead transwomen, all the lists
of the dead that no one is reading. People aren't
eating meat because Jesus died and I guess
it makes them feel like they are sacrificing
a portion of their privilege. So, they order fish
with everything on the side and substitute salad
and drink a bottle of Chardonnay and feel better, holy
maybe. I'm not pretending today. I give up pretending
today. I bought $125 worth of makeup so no one
can tell how tired I am. I never gave up hiding
or denial or meat or smoking or drinking or weeping.
The world is flat and everything is fine.

Emily Rose Kahn-Sheahan lives in Chicago where she has hosted and curated live lit shows and poetry slams for ten years. Her work has recently appeared in Columbia Poetry Review, TriQuarterly, Muzzle Magazine, decomP, After Hours, and TimeOut Chicago. Her first chapbook, *Cigarette Love Songs and Nicotine Kisses*, was published by Cross+Roads Press. Her 2nd book *Mouthy* was released on Thoughtcrime Press.

Erin Davis

Darkness

Don't tell me these are dark times.
Darkness is temporary. After all,
it is the fleeting nature of the night
that gives us the confidence
to surrender to slumber.
And I haven't slept in a week.
Don't tell me it's always darkest
before the dawn.
Sunrise, sunset and on and on.
Or that a shadow cast by a cloud
can be pushed away by a cleansing wind.
Don't normalize this. Don't say that it's
part of some natural cycle.
Life begins in the absence of light.
Seeds sprout out in the cool, dark ground
and babies are formed in the dim, wet
caves of their mothers' wombs.
They say resurrection happened
in a sealed tomb. We rest in the dark
to begin again. But I find no rest here.
Don't ascribe this to the darkness.
Don't let the daytime off the hook.
What was done did not happen 'neath
the cover of night. What we did or didn't
do, we did or didn't in the light. Our choice
was not cloaked in the hushed hues
of evening. It announced itself loudly
in the harsh tones of morning. Sunlight
is not our disinfectant. It offers no healing.
It exposes everything about us
that is ugly and unkind, then
laughs with delight when
we can't avert our eyes or seek
the solace of communal sleep.
What we dreamt in the dark was
ours to keep. But we chose differently
when the day came. We stepped out
of the tomb with our eyelids sewn open
and marched ourselves into unbearable brightness.
Don't try to soothe me with talk of darkness.

Erin Davis lives and writes in Spokane, Washington and teaches composition and literature in North Idaho. Her work has been featured in Assay: A Journal of Nonfiction Studies, and Trestle Creek Review. She has twice been a reader in Eastern Washington University's Get Lit Festival, and in 2014, her work was featured in Spokane's Listen to Your Mother show. She finds inspiration in the beauty of the Little Spokane River, the support of her family, the curiosity of her students, and the groundswell of social justice activism in the Inland Northwest.

Devon Balwit

Waving Valiant Colors

Orion stands broad-legged guard over nothing. Here
streets are quiet, children safe from most dangers. My
dog, ever mysterious, noses the perfect place to lift a leg,
the newspaper in its bag still closed against the horrors
of today and yesterday. I have not yet confronted the
day's measure of suffering or the most recent assault
by the madman who won the Presidency. No bomb
has yet exploded in any city whose name I recognize.
Black men still have two living hands with which to hold
wives and children. As far as I know, hackers have not
brought us to our knees. So as not to alarm, the freeway
whispers like surf, whisking the good people of my city
about their business. Fall continues to wave valiant colors
before yielding to chill. Full of stubborn hope, I go in.

Devon Balwit writes in Portland, OR. She is a poetry editor for Minute Magazine and has six chapbooks out or forthcoming: *How the Blessed Travel* (Maverick Duck Press); *Forms Most Marvelous* (dancing girl press); *In Front of the Elements* (Grey Borders Books), *Where You Were Going Never Was* (Grey Borders Books); *The Bow Must Bear the Brunt* (Red Flag Poetry); and *Risk Being/Complicated* (self-published with the artist Lorette Luzajic). Her individual poems can be found in The Cincinnati Review, The Carolina Quarterly, Fifth Wednesday, The Stillwater Review, Rattle, Red Earth Review, The Fourth River, The Free State Review, and more.

Robert Jensen

The election of Donald Trump reflects the failure of America. The tough question: Who is responsible? Whom do we blame?

Is the problem Trump's self-aggrandizing authoritarian charisma? Or is it really the fault of the wealthy—the top 10%, or maybe just the top 1%, or the 0.1%—who as a class seem incapable of empathy and solidarity? Or Trump voters' willingness to embrace a carnival barker rather than think critically about who really rigs the system? The Republican Party's ideological fanaticism? The hypocrisy of the politicized evangelical Christian community that suddenly decided a candidate's character was irrelevant?

The Democratic Party's preference for the three-decade-old Clinton program of privileging wealth and "experts" over an energized grassroots? The bitterness of some Sanders supporters that led them to minimize the danger of Trump? The apathetic who don't engage politically because they believe the system to be corrupt beyond redemption?

What about the failure of systems, notably of capitalism and U.S. imperialism, not only ignored by conservatives but downplayed by most liberals? The collective failure to face the everyday realities of patriarchy and white supremacy? The failure of humans to recognize the catastrophic impact of our high-energy/high-technology indulgence, with the United States leading the way to the edge of the cliff?

Wherever we drop the blame, I'm tempted to scramble to make sure it isn't too close to me. After all, I'm an activist fighting illegitimate structures of authority, but one willing to make pragmatic decisions about political choices at any given moment. I'm a teacher who brings critical perspectives into the classroom. I'm a writer who uses his limited visibility to challenge systems and structures of power.

But I can't ignore reality: I'm a failure, too. More accurately, I'm part of the great American failure. We are not all equally responsible for that failure, but we all are part of the failed American project. "America"—the country itself, and its affluence—is built on a domination/subordination logic that immiserates the most vulnerable and relentlessly degrades the larger living world. That is the America we all live in, live with, are haunted by.

America is a failed project. Trump asserts "make America great again" as a promise. I take it as a threat.

It's a bad feeling, the awareness of this failure, and I can't shake it, and I shouldn't try to, and neither should anyone else. For the next four years (let's not ponder the possibility of eight), there are opportunities for resistance that we should take up, vigorously. But let's let that bad feeling linger. There's something to learn from it.

Robert Jensen is a professor in the School of Journalism at the University of Texas at Austin, and author of *The End of Patriarchy: Radical Feminism for Men*, to be published in January by Spinifex Press. Other articles are online at http://robertwjensen.org/. He can be reached at rjensen@austin.utexas.edu.

Now You Know

The morning after the end finally began there were tears and panic and protests and proclamations. A new fear spread among us like a virus. Some hid, some posted, some trolled, while others took to the streets. It felt as if the sunshine had been unceremoniously snuffed out, and we were cast into a new nightmare, the pall of which hung over every interaction like a thundercloud. Like a swift kick to the hope. Much of what had once felt crucial was rendered suddenly trivial when faced with the prospect of internment, deportation, civil war, racial hatred, misogyny, and bloodshed. Now you know how the Germans let it go down. What to do now? Speak. Love. Fight.

Clark County Poet Laureate Christopher Luna and his wife, Toni Partington, founded Printed Matter Vancouver, and co-host Ghost Town Poetry Open Mic, the popular reading series Luna established in Vancouver, WA 2004. Luna's books include *Brutal Glints of Moonlight*, *GHOST TOWN, USA* and *The Flame Is Ours: The Letters of Stan Brakhage and Michael McClure 1961-1978*.

Janina A. Larenas

In Lieu of Not My President

In the wake of the 2016 Presidential Election, a wave of opposition erupted throughout the United States. One of the most prominent slogans used by this opposition is, "Not My President." It is intended to illustrate that over 73 million Americans (roughly 54%) did not vote for Donald Trump, but the slogan evokes a sense of non-participation and lack of responsibility that undermines the intended political message. Because we are responsible for Donald Trump. We did contribute to this moment. It becomes a sort of misplaced political mourning cry, suggesting that since we didn't vote for him we are not responsible for him. The move to turn away from that responsibility forgives us from examining the structures we participate in that allow for a Trump Presidency to exist. In a moment when people are frustrated, afraid, and heartbroken about the political state of the United States, we should not encourage a slogan that forgives them the call to political action. As organizers, as resisters, as representatives of the left, it is our responsibility to use this as a pedagogical moment, to teach people how to resist, how to demand something better, and that includes demanding something better than "Not My President."

The problem is that we haven't been offered something better. People are looking for a way to say, "Donald Trump doesn't represent my politics, we stand in opposition, we will not consent to the policies or practices of white nationalism, misogyny, religious intolerance, or homophobia." But this search fails to address how we arrived here in the first place. We need to address the systemic problem of neoliberalism, embedded hierarchical structures, the class disparities inherent in capitalism, the obvious flaws in our electoral system, and the complete failure of the Democratic Party to recognize the struggles of working people in favor of a long shift to the right. We have to acknowledge that it will take a lot more action and change than simply voting *against* someone to fix these problems. So in lieu of joining in with Not My President, we demand something more. We engage people in the streets shouting "NOT MY PRESIDENT" and intervene with "NO MORE PRESIDENTS." We open up a dialog with people in our communities to hear their struggles and together create a stronger politics. We talk about the contradictions of a nation of people voting against their own interests. We expose the myths that neoliberalism encourages about the virtues of a self-regulating free market. We do more than call our representatives. We point the frustrated, the afraid, and the heartbroken toward local organizing projects. Together, we learn how to demand something better than "Not My President," demand something better than capitalism, and when we aren't offered something better, we start building it. We don't mourn, we organize.

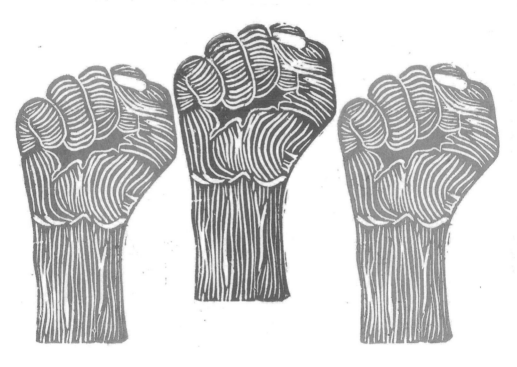

Don't Mourn Organize
Janina A. Larenas

Janina A. Larenas is a printmaker and book artist who works with a variety of mediums to create narrative imagery. Her pieces range from stickers and posters to science illustration, embroidery to zines, often merging technical crafts with fine art presentation. She is a trained California Naturalist and AAUS Certified diver, founder of Print Organize Protest and the Little Giant Collective.

Inauguration Poem 2017

Today we put your name on everything.

Today we tweak a definition,
take a word that once meant
"get the better of" and see
its connotation embodied
by a person who in every way
was less than his opponent
take the title for an office
he cannot fulfill, convert
the ultimate public service
into continual tribute
as he laves largesse
on the wealthy, on the worldly ones
he thinks are worthy winners,
following a philosophy he cannot understand
expressed in books he has never read
to resurrect an idealized way of life
that has never existed.

Today we put your name on everything.

Today we put one name aside,
for now, and cannot call
ourselves "United States"
but have to say "America,"
a selfish name, a name
ignoring those who share
our hemisphere and borders,
all America, all America,
and never us alone except
in narrow fisheye vision,
cropped in scope
but magnifying one core spot
with unrelenting focus.

Today we put your name on everything.

On every magazine we'll see your name.
On every telecast we'll see your name.

In every conversation we'll hear your name.
In every confrontation we'll hear your name.
In every institution we'll hear your name:
"The Trump White House," "The Trump
Supreme Court," "The Trump Doctrine,"
"The Trump Administration,"
"The Trump Offensive," "The Trump Casualties,"
"The Trump Toxicity," "The Trump Hearings,"
"The Trump Indictment," "The Trump Recession,"
"The Trump Depression," "The Trump Bankruptcy,"
"Trumpgate," "The Trump/Russia Connection,"
"The Trump Scandal," "The Trump Impeachment,"
"The Trump Legacy," "The Post-Trump America."
We remain anxious for "The Post-Trump America."

Today we put your name on everything.

When we see a new distrust among our working relationships,
when we find we do not enjoy the company of some of our once-close friends,
when we come to realize that we did not understand some of our family at all,
when we see everyday failure of character,
when we challenge capacity for compassion,
when our empathy struggles to sustain itself as it once could,
you will be in our thoughts.

Today we put your name on everything.

When we hear the evangelicals refer to you as an agent of God,
when we hear our former fellow congregants assure us of your godliness,
when we hear our estranged elders say that you've repented and earned grace,
when we hear our laypeople explain they've "won,"
we will not understand.

Today we put your name on everything.

When you share with us on Thanksgiving your platitudes of gratitude,
when you offer us Christmas greetings,
when you select a media-immersive church for Easter service,
when you invite us to celebrate Independence Day,
when you call Columbus the first great American,
when you lay a wreath at the tomb of the Unknown Soldier,
we will not think of those days the same again.

Today we put your name on everything.

When families separate, we will name you,
when families are kept apart, we will name you,
when sick and hurt cannot get care, we will name you,
when innocents are brutalized, we will name you,
when we fight,
when we bleed,
when we lose,
when the world contracts and segregates,
we will name you.
When we speak up,
when we stand,
when we resist,
when we resist,
when we resist,
we will name you.

Today we put your name on everything.

Thomas Alan Holmes, a member of the East Tennessee State University English faculty, lives in Johnson City. Some of his work has appeared in Louisiana Literature, Valparaiso Poetry Review, Appalachian Heritage, The Connecticut Review, North American Review, Pine Mountain Sand & Gravel, Still: The Journal, and The Southern Poetry Anthology Volume VI: Tennessee, with poems forthcoming in Zone 3, Appalachian Journal, and The World Is Charged: Poetic Engagements with Gerard Manley Hopkins (Clemson U P).

MAKE THE NOISE YOU THOUGHT YOU COULD

Rose M. Smith

The Aftermath of Purchase

Say again how much you wish you'd known
the foundations of this house
leaked in inconvenient places, held
secrets no one catalogued in deeds
and regulations.

Say again you knew the cost
but did not realize you'd be left
to pay. For every truth withheld,
every unexpected brick dug up
from front-yard scape
where fountain, porch, or bed edge
once restrained unpredicted wildness.

Say again you signed because
it was time for change—
the dog confined to his fenced-in
townhouse patio, you confined
to your sandwiched space
between immigrant and overly-quiet.

Say you've no regrets,
have a place for this remorse.
This new level of expectation.
This end to the fairy tale
of ownership, rebirth, and freedom.
Make the noise you thought you could
where no one would complain.

Rose M. Smith's work has appeared in The Examined Life, Mom Egg Review, pluck!, Naugatuck River Review, Minola Review, Main Street Rag, Snapdragon, A Narrow Fellow and other journals and anthologies. She is author of four chapbooks, most recently *Holes in My Teeth* (Kattywompus Press, 2016). She is an IT requirements analyst by day and a "somewhat well known" performance poet. Rose is an editor with Pudding Magazine, and completed a fellowship with Cave Canem Foundation in 2015.

Acknowledgments

"A Drop of Water" by James Schwartz , previously published by WritersResist. com, and in Secular, Satirical & Sacred Meditations, Writing Knights Press.

"After the Elections Went to Shit" by Keri Withington, Published in New Plains Review.

"At Risk of Drowning" by Kit-Bacon Gressitt. First published on ExcuseMeImWriting.com.

"Beautiful Beautiful Poem" by James McManus. First published in New American Writing, 2017.

"Choice" by Joseph Ross was originally published in Truth to Power, Cutthroat: Journal of the Arts, 2017.

"Fear and Loathing in Trump's America" by Andrew Solomon, originally published in The New Yorker. Copyright © 2017 by Andrew Solomon, used by permission of The Wylie Agency LLC.

"Ghazal: A Night Already Devoid of Stars" by Jackleen Holton Hookway, published in New Verse News, August 27, 2016.

"Growing Up Beside the Continental Divide" by Jane McPhetres Johnson, first published in What Rough Beast, Indolent Press, March 4, 2017.

"How To Brace For Impact" by Natashia Deón. Reprinted with permission from PEN USA.

"Incantation on the Eve of 2017" by Monica Rico. Originally published by Cleaver Magazine as part of their Life as Activism! series.

"It Begins with No" by Chiwan Choi, Reprinted with permission from PEN USA.

"Living in Trump's Soviet Union" by Gary Shteyngart. Copyright © 2016 by Gary Shteyngart. First appeared in The New Yorker. Reprinted with permission of the Denise Shannon Literary Agency, Inc. All rights reserved.

"Now You Know" by Christopher Luna, previously published on Nicholas Kristof's NY Times blog Trump Poem contest. Reprinted with permission.

"Olympia" by Jackleen Holton Hookway, published in Rattle's *Poets Respond,* August 14, 2016.

"...Only the Past, Happening Over and Over Again" by Litsa Dremousis. Reprinted with permission from PEN USA

"So Out of Words" by Marjory Wentworth. Published in Sojourners, June 2017.

"Survival Practice" by Jasper Wirtshafter, previously published by Us for President at usforpresident.org/2017/02/07/survival-practice/#respond.

"Thank you, Tennessee" by Keri Withington, previously published in Vagabonds.

"The election of Donald Trump reflects the failure of America. The tough question: Who is responsible? Whom do we blame?" by Robert Jensen. Reprinted with permission from PEN USA.

"The Offense" by Jessy Randall, debut performance in Home of the Brave at the Rochester Fringe Festival on September 16, 2017, directed by Jeremy Sarachan, with Katie Kreutter as Tasha, Anita Bartolotta as Zed, and Marie Pellet as The Voice of Authority.

"The People's Choice" by Bruce Bennett, published in The Donald Trump of the Republic, FootHills Publishing 2016.

"The Secret Ingredients of a Supervillain," and "The Orange Menace on Vacation" by Daniel M. Shapiro will appear in Menacing Hedge's spring issue and originally appeared in the chapbook, The Orange Menace, Locofo chaps, 2017.

"The spray-paint smile on the bridge is fake" by Wil Gibson. First published on Minor Literature(s)

"The Suppressed" by John Morgan. First appeared in The Yale Review and was reprinted in Spear-Fishing on the Chatanika: New and Selected Poems.

"Track 5: Green Day – American Idiot" by Gyasi Hall. Previously published by The Establishment.

"What to do while awaiting the Angel of Death" by Carmen Tafolla, Originally published in the San Antonio Express News' Poetry Column, April 9th 2017.

"When politics are thicker than blood" by Sossity Chiricuzio originally published as part of Embody, an ongoing column in PQ Monthly, November 2016.

"Whiteout" by William Trowbridge, appears in *Vanishing Point,* Red Hen Press, 2017.

"World of Made and Unmade (Excerpts)" from Jane Mead's full length book, published by Alice James 2016. Many of these excerpts also appeared in The New England Review.

Featuring art by:

Geoffry Smalley is an artist living and working in Chicago. Originally trained as an illustrator, over the years he has worked as a muralist, a painter, an installation artist, an art conservator, and a freelancer. He received his MFA from the School of the Art Institute of Chicago in 2002 and has exhibited in solo and group shows in Chicago and across the USA for the past 20 years. While his work generally plays with the interstices between sports and politics, or sports and religion, since the election of the Orange Menace he has delved deep into the grand tradition of political cartooning as a means to vent, cope, process, laugh at, scream about, point to, and create awareness of the egregious evil that has befallen our great land.

Pete Railand (formerly Pete Yahnke) is a founding member of Justseeds, a printmaker, educator, bike rider, self-taught musician and stay at home dad. Born in Milwaukee WI; raised in the north woods of Wisconsin in a town with one stoplight. Has traversed the US too many times, living and working in Milwaukee WI, Albuquerque NM, New York, Red Wing MN, Oakland CA, Santa Fe NM, Minneapolis MN, Portland OR. Recently returned to Milwaukee after a 16 year absence. Wonders when he will leave.
Currently he plays music with slow speed doomers: The Old Northwest theoldnorthwest.bandcamp.com and Milwaukee's most mysterious: Gnarrenschiff

Special thanks to artists Pete Railand and Janina Larenas who donated prints for our Kickstarter campaign. Thank you Molly Crabapple who helped get this whole project off the ground with her incredible cover art. Thank you to Kit-Bacon Gressitt for the encouragement and the promotion. Thank you Ed Dadey and Art Farm Nebraska for the space to work on our many Thoughtcrime projects. Thank you Amanda Palmer for getting even more artists involved and for being a constant supporter of art and literature. Thank you to all the Thought Criminals for supporting your press with your brilliant words and art. Thank you to all the writers and artists who submitted work to this anthology. You are The Resistance. You are who our world needs.

Thank you to my wife and daughter for putting up with the late nights, the hateful emails from Trump supporters, and all the time we spent apart while I worked on "a small anthology" idea that turned into a massive undertaking. I love you both so dang much. And thank you to co-editor and incredible human being, my friend and brother Ben Clark. I am a better person with you in my life.

Afterword

I wrote this afterword instead of a foreword because these voices needed no introduction, and because I did not intend to imply our permission for anyone's work or voice to be expressed. Numerous people requested that I say a few words though about what led me to make the book, and discuss some of the criticisms I received for doing so.

My initial goal was to gather a historical cross section of voices from as many different backgrounds as possible united in their common concern regarding the presidency of Donald Trump. From week one I received numerous complaints concerning the title. I repurposed the title, *Not My President*, from right-wing rallies I observed protesting the election of Barak Obama in 2008. To explain what the title means to me, I need to explain what the presidency means to me. We elect a president to act as the chosen public servant, paid employee, and representative of the people. In the USA, no one has more bosses than the president because the president is our servant, beholden to every voter and to the Constitution of the United States of America. When I chose *Not My President*, I did not mean Trump was not the elected official whose job is it to serve the nation. Instead, I meant to imply that as my representative, and as my employee, Donald Trump fails. He is not my public servant as he does not represent my beliefs. Furthermore he does not represent our national values enumerated in our Constitution, nor does he defend the inalienable rights from our Declaration of Independence. Instead, he represents the voices of a deafening minority of money interests and an equally cacophonous minority of voters. He truly is not my president.

Regarding those who voted for Trump: Trump, faux news, and the Republican Party bamboozled many voters into voting against their own best interests, *but* at the same time also encouraged them to vote in line with their own deep seated prejudices and fears. These fears become weapons that voters give to politicians to turn against the voting public. Many of these voters have recently learned that Trump is not their president either, and never was. Many have already suffered, and will continue to suffer under the administration they elected. I hope that when they come to us asking to join in our fight against injustice, we can find it in ourselves to allow them that, even if we cannot trust them or do not forgive them for their previous actions.

From a technical aspect, we arranged this book's sections by the lenses through which people saw this election and its aftermath. Most works, however, could have easily fit into numerous sections. We ordered each section by trying to find the conversation or unintended narrative between pieces. We placed bios directly after an author's work, because in this anthology the person and their work are of equal importance. An anthology bio tucked at the end of a book in a jumble of pages becomes easy to ignore. Here the reader must engage with the human behind the work, even if only for a moment. For similar reasons, we made a stylistic decision in the bios to only italicize works that were solely those of the author, or done in close partnership with the author, as opposed to the standard italicization of all journals, etc. This allows collections of an author's work to stand out, instead of fading into a general glob of italicized words that people often skim or ignore.

I want to remind any unelected individuals who read this anthology, that *we* are the leaders. Public servants, as in *all* elected officials, are exactly that—the servants of the public. Don't serve the servants. They serve by our permission, not the other way around. Terminology matters and words shape how we think. We would be better served if we began referring to elected officials by their true roles, and "leader" is not one of them. We aren't paying servants of the public to lead the public. If we begin to see ourselves as the leaders, and see our elected officials as true enactors of our will and not the other way around, I believe we will progress further, faster.

We will send a copy of this book to every member of the US Congress. We hope they read the work within and take to heart the voices of a suffering nation, and world.

My name is Josh Gaines and I am the founder of Thoughtcrime Press. I am a former Air Force Officer, a husband and father, a writer, and a leader. As a member of the public, I am in some way responsible for my current government/employees, even when I did not personally hire or elect them. Conscientious people lost in the 2016 election. As a community of leaders, we made or allowed some poor decisions, and that hurts. But, I can learn from my mistakes. I can do more and do better. 2018 looms. To quote Joe Hill, "Don't waste any time mourning. Organize!"

We will donate proceeds from this book to charitable organizations hurt by policies pursued by the current administration.

THOUGHTCRIME PRESS

Join us at thoughtcrimepress.com